ATTA(

A high-(   ) adventure story for kids eight years and up. When their favorite teacher suddenly goes missing and the police haven't found him, The Riwaka Gang, four country kids who love adventure, decides to get involved. Jackson, Jessica, Rangi and Sam will need every skill they have plus a ton of courage. Dangerous situations and extreme challenges confront them. But will they find Mr. Chapman? With so many impossibilities, the odds are stacked high against them. The story is set in Riwaka (Ree-waaka), a quiet, seaside, country town in New Zealand – in the South Pacific. 'A gripping, high-speed adventure story with loads of New Zealand imagery – kids will love it.' It is the first in the series of the Riwaka Gang Adventures.

WHAT READERS ARE SAYING:

"An exciting adventure story. I couldn't put it down." – Shirley"

I couldn't stop reading. It's a real page-turner with an amazing, surprise ending." – Mitchell

"A gripping, high-speed adventure story with loads of NZ imagery – kids will enjoy the thrilling escapades while learning sound values." – Cathy

"The fast pace of the story keeps interest alive as the mystery develops and the danger increases." – Colleen

"... An exciting, action-packed adventure story – relatable characters and lovely descriptions of the New Zealand landscape ... a winner." – Jo Louise"

"A cracking pace and satisfying finish make this unique New Zealand adventure story a great read." – Jean

"A great children's adventure story ... compelling reading. Good family connections and good wins over evil." — Bob

"A great story — couldn't put it down ... an Adventure that keeps you guessing. Highly recommended." – Kiwikid

"... had trouble putting it down. Exciting adventure with a good message to the children. Can't wait to read the next one." – Lesley

"I was kept enthralled from start to finish and became part of the Riwaka gang. A great story ... even beats 'The Famous Five', a favorite series of mine." — Jude

"Riveting book ... full of adventure. Twists and turns that catch you off-guard and keeps you engaged until the surprising end." — Valerie

"Will keep you on the edge of your seat ... mountains, beaches, caves and sea all close by. Highly recommend it – a must read." – Ally

Attack at Shark Bay

A Riwaka Gang Adventure

by Denis Shuker

A High-octane, rip roaring adventure
for kids 8 yrs and up.

Published by – Joyful Publishers

October 2012

This is a novel based in New Zealand. Names, characters, and places, while based on real places, are either the product of the author's imagination or are used fictitiously. Any resemblance to actual persons, living or dead, or to actual events or locales is entirely coincidental.

Copyright © 2012 – Denis Shuker.

Dedication –

This book is dedicated to
some special people in my life –

Alice Joan Shuker
My wife, best friend and life's partner.

Without her help
The Riwaka Gang would still be in my computer.

Also to – David, Catherine, Alison and Gregory

I hope you have as much fun reading this book as I
have had writing it.
– getting to know these four special people –
Jackson, Rangi, Samantha and Jessica;
— The Riwaka Gang —

Watch for the next big adventure of
THE RIWAKA GANG!

Stay in touch; for information on exciting new
books coming up – go to my website and sign up for
news of the next big adventure of

The Riwaka Gang coming soon!

Go to: **www.denisshuker.com**

CONTENTS

1. DAY ONE 8:15 AM

Jackson Curtis skidded to a stop in a cloud of gravel and dust. Jackson was tall for fourteen, with smiling eyes and a mop of ginger brown hair. He adjusted his school bag over his shoulder as he waited outside his friend, Rangi Kingi's house. He always biked to school with his best friend. Rangi's home was only a few minutes from their farmhouse. Rangi soon arrived on his bike, accelerating down their drive, then screeched to a stop alongside him.

He had his usual bright smile. "Morning, bro."

Jackson grinned. "Summer holidays sure are my favorite time of year. Can't wait for tomorrow."

Rangi nodded. "Yeah, me too. Okay, ready to go."

It was only twenty-five minutes down the valley to school. Riwaka High School served the small country community well. The two boys arrived and parked their bikes.

They raced across the football field towards the school buildings.

Jackson looked around the crowd of kids arriving. "We've got to get the Riwaka Gang together and make plans for summer."

"How about tonight after school, at your place? I'll tell the girls," Rangi offered.

"Sounds good. Okay, let's do it." The Riwaka Gang often met in the large sunroom at Jackson's family's farmhouse.

Their classroom was filling up. The two boys raced in and grabbed their favorite seats, at the back. With his Maori good looks, Rangi was popular with the girls. But he wasn't much bothered. He was more interested in sports.

Their math teacher, Mr. Thompson, arrived, frowning. The class went quiet. "Before we begin, I have two announcements. I regret it's not good news. First, the police will be around the school today. If you are asked any questions, tell them to talk with a teacher." He paused while he arranged his books on the front desk. "Mr. Chapman, your sports teacher, has suddenly disappeared. He has been missing for twenty-four hours now. The police are investigating. The other news is our new school gymnasium project has been canned. The special fund is $80,000 short. I wish I had better news for you all, on the last day of school."

Jackson's jaw dropped. He turned to Rangi. "I can't believe it. Chappy is such a reliable guy."

Rangi scratched his head and leaned back, looking out the window. "There must be a good reason why he's not here. Maybe he had to go away suddenly. Could be his family in Australia needed him or...can't imagine him just not turning up."

Mr. Thompson called the class to order. The morning went quickly. Jackson couldn't focus. Everything went past in a blur. He could only think about Chappy. What could have happened to him? Chappy was his favorite teacher; where was he?

The school was buzzing with unanswered questions. Jackson and Rangi always had lunch together on seats by the rugby football grounds. That day his sister, Jessica and Rangi's sister, Samantha joined them. They were known as The Riwaka Gang. Normally, Samantha would only answer if you called her Sam. That day, fourteen-year-old Sam sat next to Jackson. She swept back her long black hair. "Did you hear the news about Chappy? What do you make of that?"

"Wish I knew. He's been giving me special training for the school triathlon champs coming up." Jackson scowled at his beef and pickle sandwiches. "Anyone got any ideas about where he is?"

Chappy wasn't only his sports teacher, he was also a friend. There was no-one else Jackson could talk to about his problems.

Ten-year-old Jessica turned to look at Jackson and swallowed her mouthful of sandwich. "Are we going to meet at our place tonight? It's time the Riwaka Gang got organized for the holidays. Let's talk some more then." Jess was slim, fit and full of ideas – a real spark plug. She brushed back her dark blonde hair from her face. "I just feel Chappy will turn up okay. But we do need to plan what we're going to do this summer."

Rangi had finished his lunch. "Everyone kick their brains into gear before we meet tonight. It's going to be a great summer."

"You bet." Jackson grinned. Maybe things would turn out okay after all.

Lunch was over. They all hurried through the school courtyard to their classrooms. Two police officers were in the schoolyard. The crowds of kids were much quieter that day.

Jackson screwed up his face as he went back into the classroom. He wasn't so sure things would turn out okay for Chappy.

Something really bad might have happened to his friend.

2. DAY ONE 2:15 PM

Mr. Thompson called, "Class dismissed. Enjoy your summer holiday."

Rangi looked around at Jackson. "Gotta go into town for my mom. I'll catch you at your place later."

"Okay, see ya later then." They hurried across the school yard to their bikes.

Jackson could smell the tang of the sea air blowing up the valley as he whizzed out of the school gate on his bike. A good sea breeze meant great surfing and good sailing out in the bay. Rangi had helped him clean up their Hoby catamaran for summer; it was looking good and ready to go. He couldn't wait to get out on the sea with Rangi at Shark Bay again. Right now, he had things that were more important on his mind. What had happened to Chappy?

He pulled his navy school shirt out as he biked and looked around at the mountains surrounding their valley. On one side of the valley, sheep and cattle farms covered the steep hillsides, which were a fresh summer green. The mountains on the other side were covered in tall forest. Further down the valley, he could see late snow on the mountain tops behind their farm, where the hills rolled down to Shark Bay.

His mind was playing tricks on him. First it was popping with fun and summer holiday ideas. The next minute it was full of worries about Chappy. He turned right onto the road towards their farm. He'd only gone a hundred yards when he heard strange noises coming from behind the bushes at the side of the road. Jackson pulled up to listen.

"Let me go! Let me go! Help!" It sounded like one of the junior boys. He knew the next voice. It was Snyder Wratt, the school bully.

This could only mean trouble.

3. DAY ONE 2:20 PM

He pulled over closer and held his bike as he listened.

"Shut up, brat, and empty out your pockets – how much money have you got? And don't yell or tell anyone or we'll really mess you up."

Jackson was strong and tall for his age. But nobody messed with Snyder. He was two years older than Jackson, bigger and stronger.

Jackson decided he couldn't do nothing. He dropped his bike on the grass and pushed through thick, spiky, native manuka bushes. He could see Snyder in a clearing, holding a small junior boy by the feet and shaking him. It looked like he was trying to empty his pockets.

Jackson clenched his fists. "Snyder, who gave you permission to beat up juniors?"

Snyder sneered at him. "Stay out of this, Curtis, or you'll regret it."

"Let him go, Snyder." Jackson moved in closer and gave him a shove.

Snyder dropped the boy, who took off like a rocket, and swung a haymaker punch at Jackson's head. Jackson ducked easily under the punch. Using his karate training, he got in close and hammered his elbow into Snyder's ribs. Snyder screamed with pain and anger. Jackson pulled back quickly to miss another punch and caught Snyder off-balance. Now he was into this, how would he get out of it? Suddenly a massive blow to the back of Jackson's knees crashed him to the ground.

"You forgot there's two of us, cowboy." Snyder's twin brother, Benson, had been waiting in the bushes. Before Jackson could get up, the two of them took to him, punching and kicking.

Jackson rolled and covered himself against the attack.

"Does teacher's pet feel a little sore now? Maybe you should have let us join your gang after all." Snyder jeered as they ran off.

Jackson got up slowly, stretched and dusted

himself off. He was annoyed at himself. Stupid, stupid, stupid — getting caught like that. Benson must have been on guard in the bushes.

He couldn't figure out what made those boneheads tick. He ran his hand through his hair. A few bruises and sore spots but it could've been much worse. Jackson grimaced as he bent to grab his school bag.

He scrambled through the bushes, jumped on his bike and headed for home. At least he wouldn't need to see those two jerks again for eight weeks. He winced with pain as he powered down on the pedals. What could have happened to Chappy? He had to get home quick and talk things over with the gang.

It felt like he had a bruised rib. That was the last thing he needed.

4. DAY ONE 2:30 PM

Jackson scanned back down the road towards school, looking for the Wratt twins. There was no sign of them now. The Wratt twins would likely be on one of the school buses waiting to leave, about a hundred yards on his left. Further down the road he could see the painted storefronts of the Riwaka Valley shopping center. People were strolling through town doing their shopping.

Jackson always enjoyed biking down their valley. It was a good time to think about things. It seemed like he had so many problems. But Chappy's disappearance was the worst.

He turned off Riwaka Valley Road into Beach Road. Dazzling glimpses of sun flashed through dark forest trees as he biked down the valley past neighbors' farms. A chorus of tuis and bellbirds filled the valley. Before long, he could see their farmhouse and woolshed near the end of the road.

Jackson frowned as he swerved around potholes. His head was spinning. His problems were like Formula One racing cars charging around his brain. He badly wanted to win his dad's approval by getting a good placing at the athletics meeting. How could he do well without his coach? Chappy was also running in the state triathlon trials in two weeks. Where did he go? Where was he?

As he got closer to home, the bitumen road changed to gravel. He biked past the Wratts' house. Their yard was a mess as usual. Rusty car bodies and junk scattered around in knee-high grass. What an eyesore. There was no sign of anyone at home.

At last, further down the dusty road he could see their own farm gate. The fight had made him late. The gang would be waiting. He grinned as he remembered the fantastic adventures The Riwaka Gang had shared over the last summer holidays — sailing, hiking, camping and barbecue parties on the beach.

He swerved as a frightened rabbit ran across the road. The sea breeze was cool on his face. Jackson leaned forward and dug his feet into the pedals. His bike leapt forward.

Raucous barking from the farm dogs announced his arrival. Jackson did wheelies in the gravel as he turned down the drive.

"Shut up, dogs!" he shouted, as he jumped potholes and hurried down the long drive to their house. Samantha's bike was leaning against the veranda.

He thought about Rangi and when his mom had died. Rangi's dad had married again. He married Jackson's aunt, Alice, giving Rangi two new sisters — Samantha and Pania. They lived on a small farm holding just a few minutes up the valley. Sam was a great addition to their gang – always telling jokes. She was fun to be around, and so was her sister, Pania. She was eight and a great kid.

He wondered about Chappy. People did suddenly disappear and sometimes were never found again. Jackson screwed up his face. He wished he'd never thought of that. But the idea stayed in his mind ... maybe he would never see Chappy again?

5. DAY ONE 3:00 PM

Jackson dropped his bike against the wide veranda surrounding their old farmhouse. He raced inside. As he burst into the kitchen, the smell of his mom's hot cheese muffins reminded him of how hungry he was.

"Welcome home, son." His mom was carrying a tray of hot muffins from the oven. "Your friends are waiting in the sunroom." She stared at him. "What happened to you? How did you get those bruises?"

"Thanks, Mom." He winced as she gave him a quick hug. He grabbed an apple from the bench. "I'm okay. Nothing much really. Just a bit of a scuffle." He decided he didn't want his mom to worry about the fight. She already had enough problems.

"You must take care, you and your karate. Take

these muffins in with you." She smiled as she gave him a plateful of hot buttered muffins. Jackson hurried through to the sunroom.

He picked his way around the overstuffed old couches and beanbags. Large sliding windows gave expansive views of their farm and the mountains. The hot sun streamed into the room and helped cheer him up a little. Jessica was relaxing over a beanbag. Her hair gleamed in the sun.

"What've you been up to, big brother? Looks like you've been in trouble."

Samantha was watching him closely from the window seat. "Looks like ya got a black eye." Her dark brown eyes narrowed. "You've been in trouble?" She was a special friend and a real good looker with dark olive skin from her Maori heritage.

"Nothing much. Benson and Snyder had a go at me after school." Jackson rubbed his head ruefully as he passed around the muffins. "The Wratt boys got me when I went to help a junior they were working over. Guess I was a bit over-confident to go and help."

"That's an enormous admission from superman, my big brother." Jessica laughed.

The fly screen banged as Rangi rushed in. "Gidday, you all." He grinned at them as he grabbed a muffin from the table and noisily arranged himself across an armchair. "Well how's it going then? Got summer sorted yet?" Rangi was a real spark plug. With his strong build, black hair and sparkling brown eyes, he was always fun to have around.

"Yo, bro." Jackson stood up and threw his apple core out the window into a paddock. He watched as some sheep came running. He wiped apple from his mouth as he looked around the mountains behind their farm. The old Land Rover truck was parked high up in the hills. His dad and his Uncle Ben were working on fences. A large mob of sheep was feeding in the paddock just above them. They looked ready for shearing, with their thick woolly coats.

"Well not quite, 'cuz. We've been waiting for your keen brain to arrive." He grinned. "Sure is good to have mates around. There's been some shocking news today."

"Hey man, that sure was bad news about Chappy. And not getting our new gymnasium with club rooms and weightlifting rooms. But that was 'specially bad news about Chappy." Rangi frowned.

"Anybody heard any news about him...? I'm thinking we need to try and do something."

"But what?" Jackson flopped onto a beanbag with a muffin and gazed at the ceiling. What on earth could they do? Where could they even begin to start looking for Chappy? Even the police couldn't find him.

Sam was looking out the window and thinking. "You don't suppose he's back on the bottle again?"

"Not a chance! Remember he's running in the triathlon coming up soon. Also, he promised us he would stay dry. We're holding him to it." Jackson just knew they could trust Chappy.

"Yeah, he's been off the bottle more than two years now. Must be something else then." Sam bounced to her feet. "Chappy always did his early morning run along the beach. Why don't we go down and check it out? We can't just hang around and do nothing. Maybe that's a good place to start."

"Great idea, Sam. Let's go and take a look around. At least we would be doing something that could be helpful." Jessica sprang up and opened the door.

"I agree, let's go." Jackson was glad to be doing

something practical at last. "It's a good place to begin. Maybe there will be some clues. The Riwaka Gang strikes again!"

Jackson moved like lightning and beat them all through the porch door. He leapt on his bike and took off down the drive in a shower of gravel. Rangi and the two girls were soon on his tail with whoops and yells, racing each other. Sam did a three-sixty as she swung onto the road to Shark Bay.

As Jackson raced to the beach, he wondered, had Chappy been swimming alone and been caught by the current? That was unlikely. He was an excellent swimmer and he knew Shark Bay.

He grimaced. Could he have been taken by sharks?

6. DAY ONE 3:30 PM

The road ran through dense native bush and ended at a wide grassy clearing by the beach. They dropped their bikes in the long grass and scrambled up the big sand dunes along the top of the beach.

Jackson was taking a running jump from the top of a high dune when he was suddenly hit by a flying tornado. He rolled down the dune with Rangi firmly wrapped around his legs. Leaping, hollering and laughing, the others slid down the dunes to the warm, golden sandy beach below.

Jackson stood and dusted the sand off. The smell of the beach and the sea gave him a real high. He looked around. The beach was deserted.

At the end of the beach, to his right, the waves crashed onto dark, volcanic rocks below their farm. Jackson looked to his left.

Marble Mountain rose steeply from the valley floor, covered in dark forest. The Riwaka River, coming down the valley, gurgled its way through the small patch of forest at the bottom of the mountain, then surged into the ocean.

"I guess we should start at the farm end of the beach. Okay?"

Walking along the beach helped calm his worries a little. He buried his feet in the warm golden sand as they hurried to the end of the beach. The warm wind, surging waves and the cries of seagulls swooping around the shoreline brought back many special memories of summer holidays on their favorite beach.

"At last, summer has arrived." Jess celebrated by doing cartwheels down the beach. They lay in the sun enjoying the warmth, but worried about Chappy and how they could find him. The silence was broken only by the swishing of the waves and the call of seagulls circling over the sea, diving for fish.

Sam broke the silence. "What do you call a donkey with a sore leg?"

"Hop-along donkey." Jackson rolled over and grinned at her.

"No – a wonkey," she laughed.

Amidst a loud chorus of groans, Rangi jumped up. "That's too much."

Jackson added, "Time to get serious. Let's start going back along the beach. Let's spread out. It's a long shot, but keep your eyes peeled for any clues about Chappy."

"Sounds good, I'll take the sea side." Jess loved walking in the shallow water. They walked back slowly, enjoying the specialness of being together again in this lovely place. As she walked, Jess picked up several golden starfish, stranded on the sand. She threw them back into the blue-green ocean.

Jackson scanned the beach and wondered how anything really bad could happen to anyone on this beach. Not many came down to Shark Bay. Other local beaches had better access roads and didn't have the sharks they sometimes saw at this beach. But that's why they liked it so much — half a mile of empty sand and great surf. Just paradise, if it wasn't for the sharks.

He shivered as he remembered the large, dark, delta fins he had seen from his surfboard last summer. Someone had said they saw a Great White shark out there recently.

He took a careful look out to sea. White-capped waves ran out past the islands, clear to the horizon. Beautiful, and no sign of sharks. Anyhow, the dolphins kept the sharks away most of the time, especially their two dolphin friends, Moko and Oronui.

They were getting close to the dark side of the mountain at the other end of the beach. Jessica stopped. "I never like coming down this end. People say there are dead spirits living in the caves guarding this end of the beach. It's creepy."

"Don't worry, Jess." Sam put a hand on her shoulder. "We'll be okay and we'll stick together."

Jackson looked up at the mountain. He shivered. The sun was off that end of the beach early each day. It sure did look spooky with the dark forest and bush lying in deep shadows. People said there were ancient burial caves hidden in the damp, dark bush. It seemed no-one knew exactly where the caves were. Nobody wanted to go in there. He wondered if the police looked in there.

"Look! Over there! What's that?" Jess ran

towards the end of the beach and picked up something lying half-buried in the sand. They ran over and crowded around.

"Well, whaddya know, an iPod." Rangi looked around. "Nobody around right now. It must belong to somebody."

Sam gazed at it and frowned. "It looks a lot like Chappy's iPod. It's the same size with a dark blue skin like his." She looked around at them. "Could it be, he was down here on his run and lost it?"

Jess looked up at the dark mountainside above them, wide-eyed. "I'm afraid something has happened to Chappy."

"And take a look over here. Looks like there's been something going on." Rangi was down on his knees examining the sand.

Jackson went over to have a look. "Yeah, look under the loose sand, there's scuffle marks. Like some people were messing around. And look, it seems like something's been dragged down towards the sea. They've covered the tracks. See, sand has blown over the top." He wiped away some of the loose sand. Now they could see marks where something heavy had been dragged down the beach.

"Could that be someone's heels dragging in the sand?" Jackson followed the marks down to the edge of the water. "And look down here! Somebody's launched a boat. Looks like it was a rowboat. See these parallel lines running out in the water? The tide's been in since then. But it's sheltered; you can still see skid marks under the water. Must've been a big one to make such deep marks."

Sam had her hands on her hips. She gazed grimly at the marks running into the water. "Man, it sure doesn't look good."

"Funny, it feels like someone's watching us." Rangi gazed around the beach. "Can't see anybody, but I've got that feeling. I don't think we're alone."

Jackson studied the top of the beach. "I don't see anyone. This is weird. Hardly anybody comes down this end of the beach early in the morning, besides Chappy."

Sam stared at the boat marks. Then she looked around the dark end of the beach. "I feel something's fishy about this place right now."

Jackson started back toward their bikes. "Okay, let's go – this is weird. I don't see any other footprints around here. Doesn't look like the cops have been looking around either. We need to go and tell them what we've found. Let's go." He was glad to be leaving.

Rangi soon caught up with him. "I'll come with you to the cop shop. We don't all need to go, just you and me would do it."

Sam agreed. "We'll go and wait at your place."

"You bet," Jessica nodded, running to catch up.

Dark clouds came across the sun. The day had suddenly become ominous. They walked to their bikes in silence, keeping a careful lookout for other people. They didn't see anyone.

Jackson jumped on his bike. "They close up shop at five-thirty. We need to get down to the cops quick. See you girls back at the farm."

Jackson raced Rangi down the track towards town.

What had the police discovered?

7. DAY ONE 4:30 PM

Jackson stopped in the middle of town, outside the sports shop, which was next to the police station. He wiped the sweat off his face with his sleeve. Rangi pulled up alongside him and they waited to cool down. They dropped their bikes against the wall of the old, cream-painted police station and paused at the doors.

Jackson peered through the glass-paneled doors but couldn't see anyone inside. The police station made him nervous. He would rather face a bull than go in there.

Finally, Jackson pushed through the two heavy swinging timber doors. "Come on, Rangi, let's just do it."

He walked into the large entrance area with Rangi close behind. They waited quietly at a dark, stained wooden counter. The sign on the counter said 'On Duty – Sergeant Harris'.

An enormous man in a bright blue police uniform with three large shoulder stripes sat hunched at a small desk in the far corner. He ignored them as he tapped away at his computer.

Jackson rang the bell on the counter. Looking up from his desk, the police sergeant scowled at them from under dark bushy eyebrows. "What do you boys want? Can't you see I'm busy?"

Jackson shuffled his feet. "Sir, we wondered, is there any news yet about our teacher, Mr. Chapman?"

"It's not your business. We are following good leads." He paused for a minute. "It's likely he had to leave town in a hurry, or he's gone back on the bottle. Why do you boys want to know?"

Jackson pulled the blue iPod from his pocket. "Me and Rangi were down on the beach and we think this might be his iPod. We found it in the sand. There were scuffle marks in the sand like there had been a fight. Besides, Chappy made a vow to us to not go back on the bottle..."

"Listen, you two. I don't have time to listen to

children's tales. You boys go back to your play on the beach and leave the detective work to us professionals."

"But sir, it looks like something could have happened to him down there." Rangi looked him in the eyes as he spoke. "There's been some funny things going on."

The police officer rolled his eyes. "Don't you give me lip, boy. We know we can't trust Maoris. Now scram, both of you. Let me get on with my work." Then he looked closely at Jackson. "But wait, aren't you the Curtis boy?"

"Yes, sir, I am."

"We have a complaint filed against you by Mrs. Wratt. Apparently you attacked her sons after school today."

"But, sir, it wasn't that way at all. They attacked me."

"That's enough of that nonsense. We'll sort it out when I come out to your farm and visit with your parents soon. Now get – both of you."

The police officer turned his back on them and went back to his computer.

Jackson looked at Rangi and Rangi looked at

Jackson. They shrugged and headed out the door.
It was bright and sunny outside. People were
bustling up and down the street, busy with late
shopping. Some businesses were beginning to close
their doors. It was time to go home.

Jackson put a hand on Rangi's shoulder.
"Boots, don't take what he said too seriously. The
cop's a jerk."

Rangi spat in the gutter. "The man's a kuri.
Let's go home."

"Yeah, he's a dog all right." Jackson had never
seen his friend so angry.

"We'll see who's the bigger fool." Rangi slapped
him on the back. "Thanks, mate. And what about
you? Sounds like he's having a go at you too."

"Yeah, those Wratts've sure got a nerve. Let's
go."

They jumped on their bikes and headed for
home. Rangi waved to his dad in the local locksmith
store as they flew past. Black clouds were tumbling
across the sky. It was getting darker as they raced
each other back to the farm.

Jackson frowned. If that was Chappy's iPod
they'd found, and he was starting to think it could

be...maybe Chappy was in some kind of trouble. It was beginning to look like he was.

It seemed that the police weren't much interested in the evidence they had found. He beat his fist on the handlebar. Did no-one care? Chappy had gone missing!

8. DAY ONE 5:30 PM

The two boys pulled up to the farmhouse and discovered Jess and Sam had saddled up their horses, Sunny and Blacky. They were jumping barrels and low fences laid out in a ring around the paddock while they waited. The boys biked over to the fence.

Sam looked down from her black mare. "How did it go?" She looked carefully at Jackson. "Looks to me like – not very good, huh?"

Rangi spat into the paddock. "Yeah, we talked to Sergeant Harris. He's a pigheaded racist."

Jackson leaned on the fence and pulled off some pieces of sheep wool caught in the wires. "We need to have another get-together and decide if there is anything we can do. Let's meet in the sunroom in a few minutes, when you're ready."

Jackson and Rangi went inside while the girls unsaddled the horses and turned them back out into the paddock. Jackson filled a pitcher with cold cordial and found some of his mom's fresh cookies; just the thing for problem-solving. Soon they were all comfortable in their favorite meeting place, munching cookies – and thinking.

Rangi looked around at them. "You remember I said – seems like we were being watched on the beach? Us Maoris have a special sense for these things and it's usually right. There's something really fishy going on at Shark Bay."

Jackson rearranged himself on his beanbag. "You mean there was somebody down there watching us?"

"Yep, that's what I'm thinking."

"Well, what were they doing there? Why were they watching us, I wonder?"

"That's what I mean. There's something strange going on down there and I feel pretty uneasy about the whole thing."

Rangi scratched his head as he thought. "There were no cars or bikes down there so if there was somebody, they must have come in on a boat."

Sam was lying across an armchair, looking out the window. She turned herself around. "Why would anyone want to be down on the beach watching us? Maybe they were hiding in the bushes? What would they be doing there?"

Jess turned to speak to Sam. "If Rangi is right, it looks like something's going on and they don't want anyone to know."

"Well, if I am right and I think I am, it must be something secret or illegal. And, I'm guessing there must be more than one of them." Rangi was relaxing in a beanbag looking out the window as he thought.

Jackson added, "And if that was Chappy's iPod, as we think, then maybe he walked in on something and got caught. But we don't know for sure."

"But if this is all true, then he can't be visiting his family or anything else." Rangi frowned. "This would mean he really is in some kind of trouble."

Sam chipped in, "If he is in trouble, then the cops should do something about it. But it seems they aren't interested to know about it."

Jessica looked around at the others. "Well if the cops aren't going to go and check it out, someone should."

Jackson sat up suddenly. "Why not us? It's beginning to sound like a job for The Riwaka Gang."

"Sounds good to me." Rangi grinned at them. "Wouldn't do any harm to go and check it out."

Jess sat up noisily in her beanbag. "Right, but where to start?"

Jackson scratched his head. He was often the best at planning things. "I think we need to go back to the beach early in the morning, about the time Chappy usually went for his run. Let's have a quiet look around."

Rangi added, "Chappy normally went running at about six-thirty in the morning. Let's go down a bit earlier. How about we meet here at five-thirty tomorrow morning – whaddya say?"

Jackson groaned. "First day of holidays. It's my day for sleeping in!" Jackson was not usually good at getting up early. But if Chappy needed help he would do anything he could. Jessica grinned at him. "Remember brother, it's the early worm that gets the bird."

Jackson laughed. "Okay then. Let's meet here at five-thirty in the morning, wear dark clothes and bring a flashlight."

"I'll tell Mom where we're going, so they won't worry," Jess added.

Jackson wondered. What would they discover at lonely Shark Bay so early in the morning?

9. DAY TWO 5:00 AM

The alarm clock shattered the silence. Jackson rolled over and choked it. Pulling back his bedroom curtains he peered out – pitch black. Not even the moon was up. At least he couldn't see any sign of rain. His watch showed four-forty-five, time to get moving.

Jackson bounced out of bed, dressed and was soon ready to go. Grabbing his flashlight, he tiptoed down the passage and knocked on Jessica's door.

She opened it immediately. "Good morning, big brother." She smiled. "Careful we don't wake Mom and Dad." They crept down the passage and into the dark kitchen.

Jackson grimaced. He was not always in a good mood at this time of day. They had a glass of water each and stuffed their pockets with energy bars left on the bench. Jessica shivered and pulled her warm jacket around her ears as they hurried out into the quiet, dark morning. Jackson pulled his bicycle from the farm shed and waited, listening, as he munched energy bars.

The world was asleep, not even a breeze stirred the trees. It was pitch black, with still no sign of the moon. He felt a shiver run down his spine. What would they find on the beach? He knew in his heart he had to go. He had to do whatever he could to help Chappy. Maybe they would even find him back jogging on the beach?

The soft low call of a ruru, a native owl, penetrated the quietness and signaled Rangi and Sam were arriving. Several owls in the forest began answering him, filling the darkness with their haunting sounds. Rangi and Sam arrived, wheeling quietly up the drive.

"Great way to start the day!" Rangi grinned, peering out from under his hooded navy sweatshirt.

"Right, let's go – ready or not." Jackson wasn't sure he was ready. He frowned. How could they be ready when they couldn't know what might be waiting?

A light drizzly rain began to fall, fresh on their faces as they cycled down the familiar dirt gravel road to the beach. Their flashlights penetrated the blackness with yellow splashes of light on the gravel road.

Sam was the first to break the silence. "Sure is a crazy time for a bike ride." She said with a laugh.

"We've done plenty of crazy things together before." Jackson hooted as he wheeled around a large pothole. He was beginning to wake up!

"This whole trip could be a waste of time too, I wonder." Jess pedaled harder to keep up.

In a few minutes, he heard the soft swish of waves on the beach. Almost there.

Jackson turned to the others. "Reckon we need to zip up now and keep real quiet."

The only sound was the quiet crunching of their tires on the gravel road. They pulled up ten yards behind the sand dunes at the top of the beach and quietly dropped their bicycles amongst the bushes inside the forest, above the beach.

The moon was rising and began to break through scattered clouds. It lit the beach with a ghostly glow. Jackson could feel the adrenaline pumping as he wriggled quietly up over the top of the sand dunes and looked around at the beach below. The moon disappeared suddenly – he could hardly see Rangi lying beside him.

When the moon broke through again, he peered into the darkness. The cliffs were bathed in pale moonlight. A heavy morning fog was sweeping in from the sea and covered the rocks at the bottom of the mountain. He studied the mountain rising steeply above the beach. It was hidden in deep, mysterious shadows. Was there someone lurking in those shadows? He shuddered.

Soon there was enough moonlight peeping through the clouds to see along the beach. Nothing moved. It was empty. Jackson gazed out to sea. He couldn't see anything through the heavy blanket of sea fog. It seemed to extend as far out as he could see into the blackness! It looked like their visit to the beach would be a waste of time. His warm bed seemed a much better option. But they had to wait. He frowned. They must wait if there was going to be any chance of discovering what had happened to Chappy.

It sure looked like it must have been Chappy's iPod on the beach. Who else's could have been there? Was Chappy okay? What else could they do to find out? The questions kept zooming around in his mind.

Samantha pulled her dark woolen jacket around her ears. "How long will we wait?"

"Maybe we need to stay a bit longer, but its blimmin' cold." Jess shivered as she looked across at the dark mountainside. "I wonder if there's anything going on over at the end of the beach. It looks so creepy."

Jackson took a long look down the beach. "No need to worry, Squirt, I can't see anything happening."

"Stop calling me Squirt." Jessica glared at her brother.

"Yeah – go easy on your kid sister, bro, she's okay." Rangi grinned at Jackson.

Rangi stood up slowly and looked around. "Nah, doesn't look like anything's doing. But, I guess we can't be too sure yet. Let's give it another thirty. Anyone want an energy bar?" He pulled out a bunch of chocolate nut bars from his jacket pocket and passed them around.

Rangi lay down again on the sand. They

munched as they waited in the dark.

Suddenly Sam lifted her head and looked hard, down towards the end of the beach. "Listen, I can hear something." The soft crunching of their energy bars was joined by another sound. They stopped chewing and listened. Quietly at first, but growing louder, they heard the quiet creaking and slopping of oars somewhere out in the fog. Whatever it was, it was coming closer.

"Keep your heads down." Jackson felt bolts of electricity running through his body. "We need to go real carefully. We can't take any chances."

The moon disappeared behind a cloud, leaving them in darkness again. Jackson felt his heart pounding as he peered over the top of the sand dune into the pitch blackness where the beach was.

The moonlight kept coming and going through the clouds, making it really hard to see anything.

Rangi elbowed Jackson in the ribs and whispered, "Think there's something happening at the end of the beach."

They held their breath and hugged the sand; afraid the moonlight might come out brighter and reveal them. The slop of the oars stopped. Jackson heard the crunch of a boat being pulled up onto the beach. Now he could see it. It was a long white dinghy.

"Must be the one that left the marks on the sand," whispered Sam.

Two big, swarthy men stowed the oars and pulled the dinghy up on the beach about forty yards away. They marched up the beach, stopped and looked slowly around. Then they hurried across the river and disappeared into the shadows of the mountain.

Jackson waited, not daring to breathe. He whispered, "I think we've found the problem and I sure don't like what I see."

Sam raised herself on her elbows. "Okay then. They've gone in somewhere down the end. Let's go take a closer look at where they went."

"Whoops – you crazy? They sure don't look friendly." Jackson grimaced.

"Sounds like a crazy idea to me too." Jessica rolled her eyes as she sat up slowly.

Rangi looked around and scratched his ear. "Funny thing, again, I feel like there's someone watching us, but I can't see anyone around."

Jackson jumped up. "Come on then, we've got to do something. I'm going down there to take a closer look." Crouching low, he crept slowly along the side of the track along the top of the beach. Soon he disappeared in the shadows of the forest.

"We can't let him go on his own," Rangi said, and he and the girls got up to follow him, keeping in the shadows of the forest.

Suddenly they froze. A man stood on the edge of the bush at the end of the track. He was staring their way. Jackson grabbed Rangi by the shoulder. "Maybe we should wait here and see what happens." He'd hardly stopped speaking when two big men in military uniform suddenly burst out of the forest and raced along the track straight at them. Jackson's heart skipped a beat. Good grief, this was it. There was no chance to run for cover in time.

They would be caught!

10. DAY TWO 6:00 AM

Jackson had never seen such savage-looking people before. His brain kicked into top gear. The two men were coming straight at them. They only had seconds to get off the track. But there was nowhere to run to. They were easy targets. It seemed they would be captured.

Rangi suddenly leapt off the side of the track. "Come on. Quick, everyone follow me." Crouching low, he dived under a low-spreading bush at the side of the track. They piled in after him and lay flat.

Jackson peered through the leaves. He could see the men clearly. They looked mean and dangerous as they ran past in their camo army uniforms and black beanies. They kept running.

Jackson couldn't believe they had missed seeing them. He waited until the thudding of the men's boots had disappeared down the track.

Jess was impressed. "Where did you learn that one?"

Rangi whispered, "Tell you later. Right now let's move quick before they come back."

"Yep, they'll be back pretty soon." Jackson leapt up. "Come on, let's move it."

The moonlight was getting brighter. They raced into a patch of dense forest alongside the track. They were only just in time as the two men came running back down the track and stopped right where they had been hiding.

The men looked slowly around. Jackson could hear them talking. "I'm sure I saw someone down about here, somewhere."

"Maybe it was just the shadows of the forest 'coz I don't see nobody around." Their footsteps and their voices faded down the track as the men ran back towards the end of the beach and disappeared into the forest under the mountain.

The first light of the sun's rays began spreading fire, red and orange, around the sky. Jackson peered through the branches. Now he could see around the bay. The fog was still too thick to see anything out on the water.

He looked around at the others. "We need to get nippy and get out of here quick. Then get home and work up a plan." Keeping low, they crept silently through the forest. They made a wide detour through the dense forest, circling back quietly, keeping well clear of the track, until at last they arrived back where they had left their bikes.

"I'm sure our bikes should be right here." Jess was looking around slowly.

Sam went to get her bike. "I know I parked mine right here behind that totara tree near the edge of the bush." She pointed to the spot.

Their bikes had vanished!

Rangi scratched his head. "I've got a bad feeling. Something really weird is going on."

"Seems someone is out to get us. Are they invisible?

"Maybe evil spirits?

"We didn't even see them..."

11. DAY TWO 6:40 AM

Jess was shaking, and wiping her eyes. Sam went over and put her arm around her shoulders. "Okay, it looks like someone's taken our bikes. It's real bad news, especially at this time of day. But it's happened and we're going to be okay."

Jackson looked around. "Can't imagine why there would be anyone around so early in the morning. Rangi, let's check the area."

Jackson and Rangi did a quick recon around the edge of the clearing, but found nothing.

Jackson frowned. "Well we won't get anywhere just hanging about. We'd better start walking back." He led the way. Rangi soon caught up with him. Their shoes crunched on the gravel road in the quietness of the early morning. Jackson's mind raced. He squinted at the bright sun bouncing off the snowy mountaintops further down the valley.

The morning mist rose up the sides of the mountains from the valley floor. The trees were covered with a thick white shroud. The valley was deserted.

There must be some reason for what had been happening, but he couldn't think of anything. Who or what had happened to their bikes? And what were those men back at the beach up to? They sure didn't look too friendly.

Rangi scowled at a 'possum as it disappeared quickly into the trees. "Seems like we're getting deeper and deeper into problems. We need to work on a plan. The cops aren't going to help us. That officer was just a pain in the butt."

Sam agreed. "Yes. We must work up a plan."

Jackson trudged along in silence, listening to the cheerful songs of the birds celebrating a new morning. The sun was now warm on his back. "Yep, let's get home for food. We need to figure out what happened to our bikes and also what's going on at the beach."

Jessica threw some stones into the ditch. "Our mom and dad had to go into the city for the day so we can't ask them about it either."

"That reminds me." Rangi suddenly stopped and turned around. He looked excited. "I know what we've gotta do. I should've thought of this before. We've gotta go and visit our Granddad Kingi. He always knows what to do when you're having problems. My granddad will know what to do."

Rangi looked around at the others grinning at him. "You know – he's really smart. He seems to have special inside knowledge; doesn't matter what you ask him."

Jackson stopped and looked at him. "Sounds cool, Rangi. Your granddad must be an amazing man. Tell me some more about him."

"Well, he's the smartest man around. I know 'coz he's helped me a heap of times – like when they wanted to expel me from high school. You remember that?"

"How could I forget it? My best friend being kicked out of high school? It sure was a bad scene. And you hadn't done anything wrong either!"

"That's the point. My granddad understood the problem. In fact he seemed to somehow know all about it even before I told him! And he knew exactly what I should do. He's amazing. He's the Kaumatua, the spiritual leader of our tribe – somehow he seems to have special understanding."

Jackson kicked a large stone down the road and watched as it rolled off the edge of the road and fell into a deep ditch running alongside the road.

"Well, I guess he's the man to see. I'm famished. Let's go and see him as soon as we've had a bite to eat." Jackson began to smile a little. Maybe they could find an answer to their problems after all.

Jessica wasn't so sure. "Rangi, your granddad's a mighty fine man but I can't see how he can help us with those dirty crooks. They looked like soldiers. Probably terrorists!" Her lip trembled. "Did you see their faces as they ran past? They looked real nasty."

"Yep – I'm sure my granddad is the one to talk to at the moment. So let's go up the mountain and see him as soon as." Rangi grinned. It helped cheer them all up a little. Jackson was looking around as they hurried back along the road to their farm. In the distance, he could see the sun bouncing off the roofs of some farm sheds above their house. The red roofs stood out like a welcoming beacon. They should be there in twenty minutes. Everything around them looked so good and normal and yet it seemed everything was going horribly wrong.

They could always smell Long Swamp before they reached it. It ran a mile along the side of the road against the mountain. It was a stinking swamp, deep and boggy. Ten acres of swamp, full of flax bushes, decayed vegetation and millions of mozzies.

Jackson stopped. He scratched his head. "Boots, you haven't told us yet how you knew where to hide back on the track. I was so impressed. And it sure saved us from those crooks."

Rangi grinned. "It's an old bush trick my Uncle Rewi taught me. Maori warriors used to use it when they were fighting their wars. It's a special kind of bush. It's good for hiding four or five at once. Handy, eh?"

They were now halfway past the swamp.

Jackson's eyes suddenly narrowed. "Say, what's that over there – in the water?" He could see the sun bouncing off something metallic in the swamp. "Hold up for a minute and let's check it out."

Jackson forced his way through the flax bushes, down into the swamp and sloshed through the smelly, muddy water. The water was up near his waist as he waded over to check it out. "Whaddya know – it's our bikes!"

Rangi screwed up his face. "Of all the brainless tricks. How did they get here? And who threw them in the swamp?"

Jackson pulled the bikes out of the swamp. He dragged them over to the edge of the road and passed them up, one at a time. Rangi lifted them up onto the road to dry. They soon had all their bikes up on the road.

Sam had a close look at them. "Far as I can tell they haven't been damaged. Looks like we're okay to go."

"Of all the crazy tricks," Rangi growled. "Wait till we meet the guys that did this."

"It couldn't have been the crooks." Jackson was making his way back up onto the road and scratching his head. "Remember back by the beach you felt like someone was watching us? I bet there must've been someone else down there this morning. Must've been at least two or three of them too, to move our bikes. But what were they doing there? And why did they pinch our bikes?"

"That's another one to ask your granddad." Jess smiled. She unzipped her warm jacket.

Samantha suddenly looked around at them with a grin on her face.

"Time for a crackup. Two missionaries were lying in their sleeping bags on the bank of a river in Africa when two lions came down the trail. What did one lion say to the other?"

Jackson shrugged. "No idea."

"Hello! Here's breakfast in bed."

Jessica doubled over laughing.

Rangi grinned. "Nice one, sis."

They mounted their bikes and set off for the farm. It didn't take long. As they turned into the drive, Jackson emptied the mailbox and carried in the bundle of letters. The dogs had all started barking. He yelled at them to be quiet.

"Anyone home?" Jess called out as they stomped over the veranda and trooped into the kitchen. There was no answer. "Mom and Dad must have left early for the city. Seems they're never here when we need them!"

"Let's eat. I'm starved." Sam heated up baked beans and made toast while Jess looked through the mail. Suddenly she screamed and held up a letter. "Look at this! I thought we already had enough problems!"

Jackson went over, took the letter and frowned as he read the rough scrawl across the page. He read it out to the others.

"Warning. Stay away from the beach unless you want real big trouble. Stay away – or die!"

"It's signed with the mark of a death skull!"

12. DAY TWO 8:30 AM

"Who wrote that message in our mailbox? It doesn't add up. How could those thugs down on the beach have anything to do with Chappy?" Jackson looked around at the others sitting on the verandah eating breakfast.

Rangi had finished eating and was stretched out, taking in the sun. "I'm sure Chappy isn't a crook."

Sam added, "Whoever it was must have known who we were."

Jackson rubbed his chin as he looked up at the mountain-tops across the valley. "Something real strange is going on. Nobody knew we were on the beach. Those crooks didn't. It spooks me."

If it was someone else, why would they want them to stay away? It was eating at him like a worm

in an apple. It seemed there were no easy answers.
He wondered, what good could Rangi's granddad
do? His granddad lived up on the mountain by
himself. He was a great man, but how could an old
man living in the mountains on his own know
anything that would help them with this problem?

Finally he put down his plate, wiped his mouth
and turned to the others. "It's time to move. Let's
get out there and go up to see Rangi's granddad."

Rangi jumped up. "Yep, we need to get moving.
It'll take us thirty up to Granddad's cabin." They all
pitched in to clear their plates into the kitchen,
rinsed them clean and stacked them on the stainless
steel bench by the sink.

It was getting hotter. Jackson took off his warm
jacket and tossed it onto a chair. Then he jumped
down from the veranda, picked up his bike and
waited for the others.

Rangi led the way on his bike. "We'll leave our
bikes in the bush about half a mile up the road," he
shouted back to them. "There's a real nice track up
the mountain starts there."

They powered off up the road after him.

About two minutes later, Rangi did a one-eighty

into the side of the road and pulled up inside the edge of the forest. Jackson jumped a log on the side of the road and skidded to a halt beside him as Jessica and Sam pulled up in a cloud of dust. The track was hidden from the road. They followed Rangi, wheeling their bikes through the undergrowth until they reached a small clearing. They left their bikes parked under a giant native totara tree. Jackson looked up. It must have been five stories tall. Rangi led them over to a dirt track, beginning at the edge of the clearing. It led into the forest and then up the mountain. Jackson had never noticed this track before. It seemed strange, as he often biked down this road. He decided that although the track was close to the road it was always hidden by the thick bush and large forest trees.

He called out, "Rangi, are you sure your granddad will be home?"

"He's always there when I go up to see him. It's kind of amazing, seems like he usually knows when I'm coming, no matter what time it is." Rangi was walking quickly up the narrow dirt track. "Can't wait to see him again. He's a real good friend too."

Jackson glanced back to check the others were

still behind them. "He sounds like a very special man, your granddad. I'm really looking forward to meeting him. Sure hope he can help us 'coz if he can't...well I don't know what we could do."

The girls had caught them up; Samantha was now close behind him. "You wait, you'll see. Rangi's granddad is a lovely man and he really does know everything. He's got special connections." She giggled.

Jessica was looking around at the forest. She stopped suddenly. "Hold on – there's something different about this forest. Look at the carpet of flowers covering the forest floor, they're so beautiful. What a lovely perfume."

"It's quite an unusual forest." Sam stopped beside her. "I've always loved walking up here. There's always so many beautiful ferns growing alongside the path too. They are just gorgeous." They stood quietly for a moment as they looked around. The sun was streaming through tall green trees, filling the forest with beams of sunshine, lighting up a sea of sparkling green leaves.

"And listen to the birds. They sound great." Jackson was grinning. "It seems like a zillion birds are all singing at once."

Rangi had stopped and turned around. "Yep, there's a special mana in this area. I've felt it before. You can feel it get stronger as you get closer to Granddad's place." They set off up the mountain trail again. Jackson noticed that somehow, his problems were becoming much lighter as they climbed the track to granddad's cabin.

"You wait till you get to meet my granddad, he's an amazing guy." Rangi beamed.

Ten minutes later, the steep track flattened out along a high ridge with wide views across the bay.

Jackson searched around the ocean, looking for any boats. "Those crooks must have sailed somewhere out of sight. Can't see a boat anywhere." They stopped and searched the horizon but all they could see was empty ocean, dotted with islands.

Sam had sat down under a tree to listen to a bellbird's brilliant song high above her. "They must have a fast boat to get out of sight before daylight. Don't these birds sound heavenly?"

The track followed along the top of the ridge, leading slowly uphill. It wasn't long before Jackson saw a lazy spiral of blue smoke, rising above the trees. Further ahead the track widened. Then they entered a large, flat, sunlit clearing in the middle of the forest. He gazed around at the magnificent trees surrounding the clearing. Songbirds filled the air with their joyful sounds. It was like another world. Granddad Kingi's log cabin of split-timber was on the far edge of the clearing. It's large cheerful windows were smiling at them. His cabin looked out over an amazing one-eighty-degree view of the bay. A wide veranda with comfortable chairs ran around the front. It looked like he often had visitors.

Waiting in a rocking chair in the sunshine was an elderly Maori man with a mile-wide smile. He looked tall even when he was sitting down. He stood as they arrived and walked over. The skin around his twinkly brown eyes was crinkled in permanent smile lines. His black wavy hair was lined with gray streaks of wisdom. He looked like a mountain man in his faded jeans and green plaid shirt.

He greeted them with a Maori welcome. "Kia-Ora. Welcome to my patch in the mountains. I'm so glad to see you all." He enveloped each of them in a huge bear hug, giving Rangi and Samantha a special long hug. "And how are my amazing grandchildren doing?"

"Hungry." Rangi grinned back at him.

His granddad gave a huge belly laugh. "Say, what do you know. I've just cooked a couple of large pizzas and I'm looking for someone to check them out for me. Come on in."

Granddad went ahead of them into his cabin. He had to bend to avoid banging his head on the top of the door.

Jackson turned to Rangi. "Your granddad is a big man."

"Yep, he sure is. He used to play in the forwards for the New Zealand All Blacks rep rugby team. People say he was a star player."

Jackson's heart felt lighter. So this was his granddad's cabin. What a fantastic place to live. He made his way down a chipped, white marble path. Three solid timber steps took him onto the veranda. Jackson followed the others into the large front room.

A large open fire crackled happily at one end of the room, with a number of comfortable chairs waiting for them. The walls were lined with many books and family pictures. Through a doorway he could see into the kitchen. The delicious smell of freshly-baked pizza wafted through the open door.

Jackson dropped into a soft chair and grinned. "This is a great place to live."

Jessica was smiling again. "How long have you lived here Granddad – can we call you Granddad?"

"I would love you to call me Granddad." He beamed at them. "I've been living on this mountain for ten years now, since my beloved wife, Ngaire, died."

"Don't you ever feel lonely out here on your own?" Jackson looked into his eyes; they were so warm and welcoming.

"No, I never feel lonely. I always sense the presence of the Almighty One with me. My dear wife taught me about faith in God and in Jesus Christ. This is so precious for me. My faith in Jesus has given my life real purpose and meaning."

Jessica gave him a quizzical look. "But how did that happen?"

"This world's a minefield; we need all the help we can get. We need God's special help to get through. It's simple but it takes courage. Trust and follow Christ through life's journey. Get involved with your church youth group. Over the years, I've found His help is always there and His promises are true." He looked around at them all and smiled.

"Now you must tuck into these before they get cold." He had brought a large tray piled high with hot slices of pizza and fresh, homemade hot bread from the kitchen. A jar of butter and a large pot of native honey were waiting on the table. He went back into the kitchen and returned with a huge pottery jug full of hot chocolate.

Jackson looked around. There was no sign of other visitors. "Granddad, how come you've just baked these pizzas and there's no one else here?"

Rangi's granddad chuckled. "I just knew you young people were coming up the mountain so I popped these into the oven. Ah, you are probably wondering how I knew. The Almighty One, who looks after me, revealed it to me this morning. You see, He's my boss. But that's enough talk for now, eat up while this food is good and hot. We can talk some more when you're all done."

Jackson sank his teeth into hot bread dripping with yummy native honey. Scrumptious! He beamed. No wonder Rangi loved coming up to see his granddad. And Rangi had said Granddad would know what they should do. He couldn't wait to find out what advice Granddad would give them. He looked around and grinned at the others spread around the room, tucking into the lip-smacking food and hot chocolate. There was something different about Granddad's pizza. Looking through the door into the kitchen, he spotted a griddle, still hot, over a log fire and decided it was the best pizza he'd ever had.

Granddad's delicious food was soon gone. Now was the time to ask him what to do about their problems.

Would he know who those men were on the beach?

Or about what happened to Chappy and who took their bikes?

How could Granddad know anything about these problems? He lived miles away up on the mountain.

13. DAY TWO 10:00 AM

Granddad sat down in the big soft leather chair by the fireside. "Well now, where do we start? You've got a lot of questions, so go ahead and ask them and I'll see if I can help you. Rather, I'll ask my boss to help me understand your problem and what you should do."

Jackson leaned back in his comfortable old chair. Where should he begin? He turned toward Granddad.

"It all began yesterday when Chappy, our sports teacher, suddenly went missing. We went down to the beach after school where he usually goes for his morning run. We think we found his iPod in the sand. We went and told the police about it but the police officer wasn't even interested.

"So we went down early this morning to have a

look ourselves – there were some tough-looking customers down there, unloading stuff from the old caves under the cliff! They came running down the track at us and maybe they would have caught us except Rangi helped us find cover and they ran right past. It was pretty scary, I guess.

"When we went to get our bikes to go home we found they had been stolen. It's all a big puzzle and we're not sure what to do next."

Rangi added, "Yeah, and we found our bikes later, in Long Swamp, as we walked home."

They looked at Granddad. "What do you think is going on?" Sam leaned over the back of her chair. "Is Chappy okay and what can we do to find him?"

"Those caves are real spooky too. I don't like to go near them." Jessica was lying in a beanbag studying Granddad's face. "They say there's dead spirits haunting those caves."

Granddad sat quietly stroking his chin for a moment. Then he stood up, walked over to the door and looked out at the sea for a few minutes. He came back and sat down again. "Rangi knows a few old Maori tricks he learned from his Uncle Rewi. Great stuff Rangi. But you all need to know, I think these men are extremely dangerous. They'll do anything to get their own way. You must go to the police."

"We did that, Granddad, but he called me a lying Maori and chewed us up for wasting their time." Rangi scowled.

"Well then. There will always be ignorant people around." Granddad sat and thought a little longer. "Okay then, here's what you could do.

"I suggest you go and have a good look around during the day, but go slowly and quietly and stay under cover and out of sight. Rangi will show you how to walk silently through the forest and he can show you how to disappear in the forest if you need to. His Uncle Rewi taught him excellent bush skills. Rewi is one of the best bush craft teachers I know.

"But keep at a safe distance. And remember, if things are looking risky, you must pull back and make sure your parents know where you are.

"I'll be asking the Lord, the Almighty One, to watch over you and help you to know what you should do.

"As for those bad spirits in the cave, this cave was once used by Maori warriors. They buried their dead in the cave. They're hidden in a branch of the cave deep inside the mountain. You don't have to worry about that, Jessica. The Almighty One, who is looking after you, is more powerful than any other spirit beings.

"The Lord will be watching over you. So if you need help, pray, call out to Him and you won't need a cell phone."

Granddad paused while he thought. Then he continued.

"I know those caves very well. Used to play in them when I was a kid – that was a few years ago now, but they'll still be the same. The main entrance by the beach is hard to find. It's hidden by some ancient kauri trees. You have to go around a corner of some large rocks to find it.

"But there's another way in from the back. It's a secret entrance that very few people know about. To get in the back entrance you go up the river about twenty yards, climb the side of the mountain until you come to several huge rocks. Go up and around behind these rocks. You'll find the cave entrance between two totara trees.

"The track through this cave will lead you into

the back of the main cave. It's pitch black and the track through the caves is rough and rocky. You'll need a good flashlight. And watch out for the sinkholes. There's some deep ones in there and some are smack bang in the middle of the track."

"But where is Chappy?" Jackson looked at Granddad, hoping he would have the answer.

"I don't rightly know. But if you keep looking for him I'm pretty sure you'll find him. The Almighty One is your guide and protector. He will watch over you. Ask him to show you." Granddad looked around at them. "I will be speaking with Him for you all.

"Now go slowly and quietly and remember to ask the Almighty God for help. He is good and kind and is ready to help you when you ask him."

Jackson was thinking, yes, they could do it! He grinned and turned around to the others. "Well, let's go and get at it."

With hugs from Granddad, they trooped out into the sunny morning again. The hike back down the mountain didn't take long. They soon reached their bikes.

Jackson kicked some loose stones along the

road. The world was beginning to look a little brighter.

But he couldn't get rid of an ominous feeling that they could be walking into big trouble.

Would they find Chappy, or would something else go wrong?

14. DAY TWO 11:00 AM

Benson and Snyder Wratt had biked into town that afternoon to do some shoplifting.

They arrived home empty-handed.

Benson jumped off his bicycle and threw it into the long grass on the front lawn. He picked his way up the rickety wooden steps to the front door and tried to enter the house. The door was jammed, as usual. He kicked it open and cursed; about time someone fixed the door.

He looked around, then called back to his brother behind him, "There's nobody home. Hungry?"

Snyder stomped into the house, frowning. "Wouldn't matter if I was – stupid. There's never nothin' to eat anyway and didn't Mom say somethin' about Jake coming around this afternoon?"

"Stuff—we'd better disappear quick before he gets here. First let's find some money and go buy somethin' to eat." Benson was looking in jars in the pantry. Then he looked out the window. "I can see Jake's old bomb coming up the drive now. Quick, let's get outta here."

They ran through to the back of the house and out the back door. Jake Wratt was in a foul mood, which was nothing unusual. He hadn't slept much the last two days, and he hadn't had a bath the last two weeks either. He'd married their mother the last time he got out of jail and needed somewhere to stay. But now that things hadn't been working out with her, he was staying at the house of a woman he'd met in prison. He turned his rusty old car into the long grass on the front lawn, narrowly missing the boy's' bikes. The engine shuddered to a halt. He jumped out and slammed the door. Spotting the boys running out the back door, he yelled at them.

"Snyder, Benson! Come back here now, or I'll bash your brains together!"

The boys looked at each other. Benson was thinking black thoughts about his stepdad. What right did he have to come back home? He had run off with some sheila and took all his ma's money.

Now he thought he could come round any time for anything he wanted. He could smell the booze from ten feet away. "Whaddya want?" He growled.

"Haven't eaten since yesterday. First you get me some food, then show me where your mom keeps her money these days."

"There ain't no food and I dunno where any money is." Benson began to walk away, but his stepfather was too quick and caught him by the collar. He flung him around and slapped him in the face. "Don't you give me lip, boy," he snarled. "You behave or I'll give you such a beating."

"Don't beat me, Jake. You know the cops'll put you back in the can if you do that again."

"Shut up and mind your business, you stupid twit. They'll do nothin' cause you're not gonna say nothin'." He twisted his collar tight, choking him.

Benson kicked him in the shins and managed to slip away. "You're not my dad anyway...only wish my real dad was still around." He spat at him.

Jake screwed his face into a snarl. "Boy, you're in for a real hiding. You didn't know how lucky you were that I came along after your pa died. Your mom needed someone to look after her." He picked up a stick and raised it over his head.

"Put that down, Jake. What are you doing around here anyway?" The boys' mom had arrived on her bike. She was a frail-looking lady but had an iron will. Jake saw the steely look on her face and threw the stick aside. "Just called around to see how you doin', Betty, and wondered if you could lend me some money."

She glared at him. "You've been drinking again, Jake. Don't you come around here sozzled or I'll call the cops. You know you're supposed to stay away."

"Aw, come on, Betty. I don't mean no harm."

She pulled out a bag of groceries from the basket on her bike and went inside. Jake and the boys followed her in. Their mom pushed aside a pile of dirty plates on the kitchen table and put the bag down. She took out a packet of cookies. "Here, take some of these and get on your way, Jake. You know you shouldn't be around here."

"I need money, Betty." He went over to the door and shut it. "Give me some money now quick and I'll be on my way."

Benson and Snyder looked at each other and started walking towards the back door.

"You boys stay here. I wanna talk to you two."

Their mom went over and picked up the phone. "Go now, Jake. I'm calling the cops."

Jake's face changed into a dark scowl. He picked up a broom and advanced towards their mom. "That's the last time you gonna call the cops on me." He beat her on the head twice with the handle. Their mom staggered and fell to the floor, and didn't move. Benson and Snyder raced over and tackled Jake to the floor but he was too strong for them and he began to beat them as well. Then Snyder slipped out of his grip, grabbed his mom's iron from the table and threw it at Jake. The iron hit Jake behind the left ear. He fell to the floor, bleeding and moaning.

Benson looked at him for a minute. "D'you think he's dying?"

"Naw, no such luck. But we'd better call the cops anyway." Snyder picked up the phone and dialed, while Benson went and tended to their mother.

15. DAY TWO 1:30 PM

The Riwaka Gang arrived back at the farmhouse to meet and plan.

Sam was the last one into the sunroom. "Knock Knock."

"Who's there?" Jackson grinned.

"Amos."

"Amos who?"

She raced over to Jackson and pinched his arm. "A mosquito."

"Ow, you got me that time," Jackson laughed as he rubbed his arm.

Rangi leaned back on a beanbag and looked over at Jackson. "Okay, what's our next move?"

Jackson was studying a large bush fly crawling around the window. "I reckon we should go back to the beach and check out that secret back entrance to the cave your granddad told us about."

Rangi nodded. "Maybe at the same time we could scout out what those men are up to down there."

Sam looked at her brother. "Rangi, you sure have such radical ideas! But I agree and let's go down there now while there's still some daylight."

"We need to stay out of sight," Jackson warned.

"It's okay, we'll be safe. I'll bring my shanghai." Jess smiled brightly at him.

They collapsed in a heap of laughter.

"Bring it anyway. You never know if it might come in handy." Jackson grinned at her.

On the way to collect their bikes, Jess picked up a few stones and dropped them into the pocket of her jeans.

This time they arrived quietly at the beachside. Jackson went ahead and got cautiously off his bike ten yards from the beach. He carefully scanned the beach. There was no sign of anyone around.

After a few minutes, he waved to the others that it was safe to come. They followed him, wheeling their bikes quietly over the grassy clearing and further into the forest.

This time they hid their bikes in a thicket behind large trees. Sliding slowly and quietly up behind the sand dunes at the top of the beach, they gazed around.

The beach looked empty. But they knew it wasn't.

16. DAY TWO 2:30 PM

They lay at the top of the beach on the warm sand for a long time, just watching and listening. Rangi tapped Jackson's arm and whispered, "Look, over there near the edge of the bush. Do you see anything?"

Jackson watched closely for a while. Then he saw a small flash of reflected sunlight – something metal?

There must have been a guard on duty hiding in the bush.

"Okay, we need to circle 'round through the bush' and come out up the mountain, further up the river, out of sight from the beach. The river goes around a bend out of sight from the front entrance into the cave. If we come out of the forest behind the bend we should stay out of sight.

"Rangi, how about you go ahead – you're the best at bush tracking."

Rangi pulled back slowly from the sand dune. Crouching low, he disappeared into the forest. They followed him, creeping through the thick undergrowth, and soon caught up. Rangi showed them how to walk silently through the forest; and how to disappear amongst the trees. Jackson was impressed by Rangi's skills.

"Your Uncle Rewi must be a good teacher." He grinned at him. Jackson looked up at the treetops about thirty feet above them. The forest was as silent as the sunlight shining through the trees.

The birds had gone quiet. Rangi stopped and waited every few minutes. "We need to make sure we don't disturb any birds. If they fly up suddenly, they'll give us away."

Jackson could only see ten feet ahead through the dense forest. He hoped Rangi knew where they were. No wonder people got lost in forests.

They had been trekking through the forest for some time when Jess whispered, "Are you sure we are on the right track? I can't see anything through the trees."

"No worries." Rangi grinned back at her. "I know exactly where we are, should be at the river in two minutes."

They came out on the riverbank exactly where they planned. Jackson led the way across the small river. Tumbling down from the snowy mountaintops, the water was icy cold and almost knee-deep. Tall forest trees hid them from any guards downriver. The rushing noise of the river covered any sounds made by loose rocks rolling under their feet as they crossed.

Jackson climbed up onto the other bank and sat in the sun on a large boulder. Rangi was close behind. He grinned. "Time for a break. Let's stop and thaw out."

"Great idea, Boots." Jackson took off his track shoes and sat down next to Rangi, rubbing some feeling back into his feet.

Jessica sat down beside them. "Jackson, why do you call Rangi 'Boots'?"

Jackson looked around at Rangi and grinned. "Gosh, I don't know. I can't remember. I've always called you 'Boots', haven't I?"

Rangi was grimacing. "When I was little, my

mom complained because I often left my farm boots by the back door. I thought they smelled real good. But everyone else had a different opinion! So the name 'Boots' has stuck since then."

Samantha buried her head in her hands, chortling with laughter. Jackson thought she looked really pretty sitting there by the river. But he would never tell her that.

He looked up at the thick bush and forest climbing up the mountain above the river. "Boots, you got any idea where those big rocks are your granddad told us about?"

Rangi studied the area for a few minutes. Then he looked back and grinned. "Yep, there's a small gap in the forest up on the right. I think the rocks will probably be in there." They made their way slowly and silently, up the hill through the thick undergrowth.

Rangi was right. Jackson found the gap between two large trees. He climbed up and discovered several giant rocks buried in the bush. Circling around behind them, they found a wide crevice in a marble slab on the side of the mountain. It was big enough for two of them to squeeze through at once.

Jackson carefully slipped through the opening with Rangi close behind. He shone his flashlight down into the cave. There was a two-foot drop onto the cave floor. He carefully lowered himself down and found himself inside a huge cave.

He turned off his flashlight. It was so dark he couldn't see his hand in front of his face. The others came in also.

They all stood and waited until their eyes got used to the darkness of the cave. Pulling out his flashlight again, Jackson shone it around. He could see a large number of stalactites hanging from the cave roof, ten feet above them. Some of their tips almost touched their heads.

The floor of the cave was rough and uneven, covered with stones and boulders. There were a number of stalagmites rising like sentinels around them.

Jackson turned to the others waiting in the darkness. "We need to go real quietly now. Any noise will carry down through the cave and give us away. How about me and Boots go and look around while you girls wait back here to guard the entrance for us?"

Jessica stood up. "I hate going into caves, 'specially this one. It's spooky. I'd be glad to wait for you out there in the sun."

"Me too. I'll wait out there with Jess," Sam nodded.

So it was decided.

Jessica and Sam returned outside to wait, while Jackson and Rangi made their way slowly and silently down into the depths of the cave.

Jackson would rather have stayed back too but he knew he must find Chappy, wherever he was. But what would they find inside the mountain?

Did this cave still go through to the back of the main entrance as Granddad remembered it? Or had something happened to block it and stop them and their plans?

There was only one way to find out.

The two boys crept into the blackness.

17. DAY TWO 3:00 PM

Jackson soon discovered they couldn't rush through the cave. The floor was covered with rocks. His flashlight helped but the blackness of the cave quickly swallowed up the small pool of light. He crept forward, watching his feet, when he suddenly collided with something very solid.

The roof of the cave had suddenly dropped down to head height. It was difficult to see very far ahead, as the cave often turned corners as it wound under the mountain. He banged his head on the ceiling several times. Sometimes they had to slalom around large limestone stalagmites rising from the floor as well as watching out for the ones hanging from the roof. Jackson thought it would be a really fun place to be, if he wasn't so nervous about what might be waiting further down the cave.

Rangi went ahead for a while.

They had just rounded a corner when he suddenly stopped with his arm held out to stop Jackson from passing.

Jackson banged into him. "What's up?"

Rangi pointed his flashlight at the floor. Jackson could see four huge black holes in the floor further down the cave. "Must be the sinkholes Granddad warned us about," he whispered.

Two were more than four feet across. Jackson was mighty glad Rangi hadn't been watching the roof when they walked around that corner. He could have easily walked into one of them! He shone his flashlight down into one. He couldn't see the bottom.

"They look like they're pretty deep."

Rangi nodded. They circled carefully around the sinkholes and continued further into the cave under the mountain. The track kept twisting and turning around corners. In some places, they had to climb over piles of rocks left from rock falls. At one place, Jackson looked up and shone his flashlight at the ceiling. He could make out the faint glimmer of light on stalactites hanging from the cave roof high above them. In some darker areas he could see the bright light of thousands of glowworms hanging from the roof. Otherwise, it was pitch black. He hoped their batteries would last.

He reckoned they must have been going about twenty minutes when they both suddenly stopped and stood quietly listening. They could hear voices drifting back from the darkness ahead.

"Stupid idiot – you put the fire out." The rough voice came loud and clear down through the cave. They crept forward slowly. Soon they saw a glimmer of light coming around the corner of the cave. Shielding their flashlights with their hands, they crept on. As they reached the corner of the cave, they turned their flashlights off. Jackson moved slowly forward, keeping low until he could see around the corner. He hugged the ground. Rangi leaned over him.

He looked into a huge cavern. The roof must have been twenty feet high.

Five men sat on crates on the other side of the cavern, about thirty feet away. He had a good look at the men. They looked rough and cruel. Three of them were older, two with dark bushy beards. The other two could have been in their twenties. Except for one, they were wearing military fatigues and boots.

Several lanterns were hanging from hooks on the walls, giving a flickering light as the men sat eating from metal dishes. One of the younger men got up and began poking at a small, smoking fire with a blackened billy hanging over it. He blew into the wood, blowing up ashes and smoke, until at last flames burst up and in a few minutes the billy was boiling.

"Ya dummy. Stop blowing all the ashes this way," the older man snarled at him. This was the voice they had heard as they came down the cave.

The other young man picked up a sack and fanned away the smoke. Then he reached into a large wooden crate sitting on the floor, took out mugs and set them on a wooden slab. He poured hot drinks from the smoky old billy, then rummaged around in the crate until he found a packet of cookies and passed them around with the drinks.

There was something familiar about one of the older men.

Jackson gasped. It couldn't be. He was wearing old jeans and a gray flannel shirt. Then he turned his head toward them. The two boys could see him better. It was hard to tell in the dark, smoky cavern, but he sure looked a lot like Sergeant Harris from the police station!

Jackson could see a stack of large yellow wooden crates not far from where the men were sitting. He peered at the warning signs on the side of the crates.

"Boots, it looks like they've got crates of explosives in here. I think they must be terrorists!"

Rangi looked grim. "Yeah, it doesn't look too good. And was that Sergeant Harris from the cop shop we saw!"

"Not sure. Can't be – what would he be doing in here?" Jackson scanned around the dark corners of the cavern. There was no sign of Chappy anywhere. What a huge disappointment.

He could see another cave leading out on the other side of the cavern. It was larger than the one they had come down. He guessed it was the cave that led out to the beach. The other end would be where they had seen the man standing on guard.

"I'll take a mug out to Hank." One of the men got up and walked out through the other exit with a steaming mug and some cookies. One of the others turned to his mate.

"Okay, I'll be glad to get outta' here tomorrow, only six more crates to go. We're gonna make our fortunes on these crates of stuff. All that lovely money. What're you gonna spend it on?"

His friend took a big sip of his drink. "Start a new drug company." They rolled on their seats with laughter.

"I'm gonna take a walk." The first one got up and started walking across the cavern.

He was coming straight towards Jackson and Rangi, crouching in the shadows.

18. DAY TWO 4:00 PM

"Quick. Think of something." Rangi looked around frantically for cover.

"Come on. Quick and quiet." Jackson slithered into a crevice in the wall just behind them. The crevice was only three feet deep, but the man was not carrying a flashlight.

They crouched in the darkness, holding their breath as the man walked past them. He was so close that Jackson could have put out his hand and grabbed his leg. He walked past them and disappeared down the cave they had come in. He returned a little later, sat down by the fire and picked up his drink again.

Jackson signaled Rangi and they crept back through the cave the way they had come. The sinkholes were hidden by a bend in the cave. They were hard to find on their way back down the cave. They circled carefully around them. Jackson marked the place with a small rock cairn at the side of the cave.

Jackson came out of the cave rubbing his eyes and blinking in the bright sunlight. He was in a bad mood. They hadn't found Chappy. He looked around but couldn't see Sam or Jess anywhere. Soon Rangi clambered out of the cave and they scrambled down through the bush to the river. The girls were waiting under the tall forest trees on the river bank.

Sam got up as they arrived. "Glad you both made it out safely."

"What took you so long?" Jessica laughed.

Jackson scowled. "Don't be an idiot, Jess. We had to go real slow."

"Come on, brother. I was only joking."

"I get sick of your silly jokes." Jackson sat on a log, frowning at the ground.

"Well, I get sick of you always getting onto me. I'll see you at home."

Jessica stormed off and crossed the river. She soon disappeared into the bush.

They sat in silence, listening to the river and birds singing in the trees.

Sam was the first to speak. "Uh-oh. That was not in the plan."

Jackson stood and stretched. "Yeah, guess I blew it. I sure have problems with my sister sometimes."

Sam looked at Jackson. "I think she's not always the problem and you need to own up and apologize to her."

Jackson gulped. Now he felt guilty as well as angry and upset.

He thought for awhile. "I guess you're right, Sam."

Rangi winked at Jackson as he grinned at his sister. "I guess it happens to all of us at times, bro. Well, we'd better get back and work up a plan."

"Yeah – we can't think straight on an empty stomach." Jackson grimaced. He felt bad about jumping on Jessica like he had.

Now he was in a real fix. His problems were only getting worse.

19. DAY TWO 4:20 PM

Jessica made her way back toward their bicycles.

Keeping a good distance from the beach, she hurried back, determined to put space between herself and Jackson. She blinked back tears as she walked deeper into the forest.

Eventually she found the road and then backtracked to the clearing where they had left their bikes. What a relief it was to find her bike still there. She was angry at Jackson. She was sick of him treating her like a child.

Just because he was stronger and older and could run faster, didn't mean he had the right to treat her like a child. There were times when she had better ideas than he did, especially when it came to solving problems. She scanned the clearing slowly. No sign of anyone else in the area. She got on her bike and headed back towards the farm.

She was deep in thought as she biked home. Jackson was alright most of the time, but sometimes he got a bee in his bonnet. When that happened, he sure was hard to live with.

What had upset him this time? He could be such a pain. She hardly noticed the birds singing in the forest alongside the road. Their mom would be home from the city soon. Maybe they could talk. As long as their mom hadn't been drinking again. Life would be so good without all these problems.

She sighed and thought about Rangi's granddad. He was a good man. Maybe she should go and talk to him to get his ideas about all this. There must be some answers. Maybe she should reach out for help to this God he told them about? She decided she would.

She arrived at their gate and biked down the drive to the house, ignoring the barking dogs. Suddenly she stiffened. Something wasn't right. There were two strange-looking old bikes lying on the ground in front of their house.

"Gidday, Jessica. Is Jackson and Rangi with

you?"

Jess jumped with fright. It sounded like one of the Wratt boys. She turned her bike around and started back down the drive toward the road. Benson jumped out of the bushes in front of her and held up his hand.

Jessica screamed. "Don't you touch me."

"It's okay, we won't hurt you. We've just come to talk."

"I don't believe you. You boys always mean trouble. Now get out of my way." But Benson didn't move.

His brother Snyder called from the front lawn. "Jess. We've come in peace – honest. Please let us talk."

"You just want to bash my brother up again. I don't trust you."

Snyder walked over. "We're real sorry about that. We came to make up and talk about something that's going on down at the beach."

When she heard this, Jess pulled over by the hedge along the side of the drive and looked at them. Benson didn't look like he was here to make trouble and maybe Snyder looked a little more friendly than usual too. Perhaps it was safe to stop and listen. Anyway, the others would be arriving soon.

She got off her bike but kept it between her and the Wratt boys. "So what is there to talk about?"

Snyder walked over. "Our stepdad is helping some people doing stuff down on the beach. He got us into helping them too. Now we're worried about what's going on and want to talk about it with you and Jackson. Is he here?"

Jess looked down the drive. "He'll be here pretty soon. What's this all about anyway?"

"Can we wait until he gets here? Trouble is, we don't know who else we can talk to. We need to talk to someone we can trust. Jackson is brainy – he'll have some ideas on what we should do."

Jess felt confused. After all that had happened that day, how did the Wratt boys fit in and what were they up to? She decided she needed to play it safe.

"Okay, you boys wait on the veranda. The others will be here in a few minutes."

She went inside and locked the door.

20. DAY TWO 4:30 PM

Jackson was thinking over what he would say to Jess as they biked back to their house. Rangi and Sam were biking alongside him giving suggestions.

Sam knew how Jess was feeling. "You just need to say you're sorry and promise to treat her well in future."

"I guess you're right. I'll just do it." Jackson felt a little easier. He knew it was the right thing to do – but why was it so hard to say it?

Rangi had gone ahead down the drive and called back. "Hey, Benson and Snyder are here."

"Good grief – and I thought we already had enough problems! What's going on?" Jackson skidded to a stop by the veranda.

He turned on Benson and Snyder, waiting by the veranda.

"What are you two doing here – looking for more trouble?"

Sam and Rangi came over and stood with Jackson.

Benson frowned. "Look, we're real sorry about what happened at the school and we want to make it up to you – okay?"

Jackson looked around. It must be a trap. What were they planning?

"Look, I don't know what you guys are up to. You're not welcome here."

Snyder shrugged his shoulders and looked at Jackson. "Jackson, we're being straight with you. We mean it. 'Sides, we want to talk with you guys about some trouble that's going on down at the beach."

When they heard this, Jackson, Rangi and Sam looked at each other. Their jaws dropped.

Rangi put his bike down. "Okay, what do you two know about any trouble at the beach?"

"Our stepdad's in on somethin' with some crooks down there and he got us to get them supplies from the supermarket. They paid us okay – but we're not happy about it all and we're kinda scared about what's going on." Benson stopped and looked at Snyder.

Snyder added, "Yeah and I know this sounds crazy, but we don't know anyone else we can talk about it with. We can't go to the cops. We're already in enough trouble with them."

Jackson, Rangi and Sam looked at each other. Sam had her hand over her mouth.

"Well how about that." Jackson slapped his thigh. "This really beats all. How do we know you're not just having us on?"

"No – we're being really fair dinkum."

Jess came out of the house and joined them.

Jackson decided they had better listen to what the Wratt boys had to say, so he turned and faced them. "Okay, we'll give you the chance to say what's on your mind." He walked up onto the veranda and pulled out chairs into a semicircle. They all trooped up and took seats. The two boys faced The Riwaka Gang. Jessica went and got drinks of chilled water. Soon they were ready to talk.

"Well, okay, what have you got to say?" Jackson could hardly believe what was happening. Did they know something about Chappy?

As Benson leaned forward, Jackson could smell his bad breath. "It started when Jake, our stepdad, came outta' prison. He met some guys in the can with connections. Now he's got into helping this gang, who've been bringin' stuff and storing it somewhere inside the caves down at the beach.

"That's all we know. We took their food and stuff down, got paid and left. It's just that...well we know they're up to somethin' real bad and we don't want to be part of it anymore."

"Yeah – and Jake's a real mean man. He'd kill us if he knew we're talkin' to you guys." Snyder scowled. "And we're real sorry for dropping your bikes in the swamp too."

Sam leapt up with her hands on her hips. "So you're the dirty, rotten kids who threw our bikes in the swamp. You stinking bike thieves - and I suppose you're the ones who wrote that letter too! And now you want us to help you!"

"We'd just collected our money in the morning and were heading home, when we found your bikes down there. Thought that might scare you away from the beach. There's real trouble going on down there."

Sam looked at them. "Huh. Well it certainly wasn't appreciated. So what do you want us to do?"

Benson and Snyder looked at each other. It seemed they hadn't thought much about it. Snyder turned to them. "I guess we don't want to get into trouble. If anything goes wrong, Jake will go back in the can and maybe we could go there too. We're wonderin' what to do."

Jackson was hoping they could give him a clue at last. "Has this got anything to do with Chappy?"

Snyder studied the floorboards. "Nope, didn't see nobody else down there 'cept the crooks – we met them on the beach. Dunno about Chappy – wish we did."

Jackson leaned back in his chair. He wondered if they were being straight with them. "You boys are already in trouble. Helping crims means you'll get it, when they get caught. Best thing you guys can do is to back out. Keep out of trouble. Stay away. Don't help them anymore. Maybe you could ask your stepdad if he knows if they're holding any prisoners and let us know." Jackson wasn't sure how much they could trust the Wratt brothers. He looked at Rangi.

Jackson turned to Benson and Snyder. "If you guys find out anything about Chappy, we want you to let us know right away, okay? We're looking for him."

"Sure, if we hear anything we'll let you know." Snyder stood up.

"Yeah, if they've got Chappy we want to get him out of there." Rangi frowned. Rescuing Chappy from a bunch of crooks seemed an impossible task.

"Sure. We'll do what you said and thanks you guys. Hope you can find Chappy, he's a good guy." Benson and Snyder picked up their bikes and turned to go.

Snyder called over his shoulder, "I'd watch out for those crooks down on the beach if I were you. They're a mean bunch."

21. DAY TWO 5:00 PM

Jackson watched them disappear down the drive. "Well what do you know? I would never have guessed we'd ever see those two in our drive, except to cause trouble. Coming to apologize like that, knowing the trouble they have with their stepdad – I almost feel sorry for them."

Jess was moving inside toward the kitchen. "Well that helps explain a few things. Okay then. What's the next step besides food?"

"Yeah, let's eat." Jackson looked out across the hills as he thought about the situation. "Reckon we need to find out some more about what's going on down at the beach. I wonder what kind of boat they're using. Seems they bring it in close to shore in the mornings to load up those crates of explosives we saw. Reckon they must be terrorists."

"Was that really Sergeant Harris you saw in the cavern?" Sam was looking at them in disbelief.

"I wish it wasn't, but we both saw – and it looked like him, eh, Rangi?" Jackson was scratching his head.

Rangi's eyes narrowed. "Yeah, it was him all right, the dog. No wonder he didn't want us messing around near the beach. Whatever is going on, he knows about it."

"What are we going to do now?" Jess had put aside her troubles with Jackson.

"I'm thinking we should go down there in the morning and have another look." Jackson looked around at them. "Seems it's the only way we'll find out what's happened to Chappy."

Rangi was looking at his watch. "Yeah, you're right. We'd need to meet here real early, say four o'clock tomorrow morning. And I'd like to take a look at their boat if we get a chance."

Sam groaned. "For Chappy, I will do it." Sam was not good at getting up early. "Sun comes up at seven o'clock. Do you think that's enough time?"

"Yep, let's meet here a little before four in the morning then."

Jackson was mentally checking off their requirements. "We need flashlights and energy food."

"Better wear swimming trunks too. We might need them." Rangi was a champion swimmer.

Just then he heard his mom busy in the kitchen. She had arrived back home.

"Sounds good to me." Jackson went into the kitchen, drawn by the smell of hot chocolate and the cookies his mom was preparing for them. "Mom, it's a real mystery – what's going on down on the beach at the moment. We're going to get up early and take a look at what's happening down there."

His mom turned and looked at him. "What's going on down at the beach?"

"We're not really sure, Mom. Something's happening. We think we'll go down early and just watch to see what it is."

His mom wiped her hands on her apron. "Well, you make sure you all stay out of trouble now. Dad's busy on the farm all day tomorrow and I'll be working in town. Remember to feed the dogs when you get home."

Jackson took the cookies and the drinks into the

sunroom. He swallowed hard as he thought about what he was going to say. He waited until the others were quiet.

"Jess – I want to say I'm real sorry for the way I spoke to you before and I want to do better in the future. Will you forgive me?"

Sam and Rangi looked at each other and grinned.

Jess turned around toward Jackson. She looked like she was in shock.

"Forgive you? Fabalastic! I never thought I would hear that from my big brother. It's music in my ears. We were told in Sunday School that's what we must do. Of course I do."

Somehow, Jackson felt a lot better now that he'd said it. "Well, thanks – that's a relief." For a few brief minutes, they all laughed and relaxed in the sunroom drinking their hot chocolate and munching his mom's cookies. But there were more important matters to consider.

Finally Sam got up and headed for the door. "Rangi, time we got home to help Mom fix supper. It's been quite a day."

"No late night TV tonight, big brother!" Jess

grinned at Jackson. "Need to hit the sack early to be up with the 'possums."

"Yeah and I wonder what we'll see down there tomorrow."

He wondered, was that Sergeant Harris they saw in the cavern?

If it was– 'what was he doing down there? There was something mysterious and disturbing about the whole situation.

Would they find any answers in the morning?

Or would it only get worse?

22. DAY THREE 3:45 AM

Jackson was awake before the alarm went off. He checked his watch, killed the alarm and dressed quickly, wearing swimming trunks under his jeans. He couldn't remember when he had been up that early. He knocked on Jess's door and they went out to the kitchen. Their mom had left plates of honey granola and energy bars for their breakfast. They ate quickly in the silence of the early morning.

Jackson collected some more energy bars on their way out of the kitchen. Their jackets were waiting on the veranda where they had left them ready the night before. Quickly pulling them on, their flashlights cutting through the morning darkness, they hurried over to the farm shed to collect their bikes.

Jackson picked up a long piece of strong black

baling twine from the shed and stuffed it in his pocket. It could come in handy. It was a calm, still morning with misty fog hanging around the valley. They didn't have to wait long. Again came the quiet call of a ruru and soon two beams of light came down the drive as Rangi and Sam wheeled in.

Rangi pulled up alongside Jackson. "A new day – a new adventure. I wonder if we'll see a boat out there today."

"Hope so. I'm keen to go take a look."

"Let's get down there and see what's up on the beach this morning." Sam leaned over her handlebars as she zipped up her warm black jacket, impatient to be going. She led the way down the drive with Jess biking alongside her.

Jackson followed them with Rangi close behind. It seemed strange biking to the beach in pitch-blackness. Nothing moved. Nobody was around.

Soon some patches of moonlight began peeping through the clouds. He had glimpses of the forest trees in the pale moonlight, shrouded with morning mist.

They pulled up silently about ten yards behind the sand dunes and walked their bikes into the forest. This time they went a little further into the forest and hid their bikes behind some bushes.

Jackson led the way as they crept to the top of the dunes above the beach, lay down and watched. Except for the quiet swishing of the waves, the beach was silent. The others crawled up beside him. Heavy mist was hiding anything on the water.

The beach was empty and mysterious. The mist lifted slightly as they waited and Jackson glimpsed the misty outline of a large boat waiting offshore. "Can you see that boat out there?"

Sam had sharp eyes. "Yep, there's something out there about two hundred yards offshore. Looks like quite a big boat. There's light coming from one of the boat's front portholes."

The mist drew back a little more, then closed over again. Now they had all seen it. The boat was about the same size as the fishing boats moored at the local wharf, but more streamlined. It looked fast.

Jackson couldn't see anyone on the deck. The mist came down further, much thicker now. It was so thick he couldn't see the bottom of the beach. But

they had seen the boat. Now they knew where it
was.

They lay quietly at the top of the beach, waiting.
It wasn't long before they heard the dinghy
approaching the beach.

As the mist cleared, they watched as two of the
crooks arrived back from the boat, pulled the dinghy
up the beach and marched quickly into the cave.

"Okay, I reckon they are going in for two more
crates to load on the boat. I figure it will take them
quite a while to get two more of those big crates, one
at a time, out on the beach. Then they've got to load
them into the dinghy, launch and row out there to
the mother boat." Jackson rubbed his chin as he
thought. "I reckon we've got a good thirty minutes.

"Boots – I think we should go out and check the
boat for Chappy– are you okay to go? Let's move
now," Jackson whispered.

"Ready when you are." Rangi grinned. The boys
quickly stripped off to their bathing trunks.

It began to rain gently.

Jackson turned around. "Where do you girls
want to wait for us?"

Sam and Jessica whispered to each other.

"We've got our slickers, so we'll pull back into the forest and wait under the trees. When they launch their dinghy to go back out to the boat we'll flash you three flashes."

"Great idea." Jackson could feel the adrenaline pumping – were they about to go into the lion's den? What would they find on that boat?

The boys left their clothes in a bag under some bushes and crept down into the water. The sea was warmer than the cool rain on their backs.

"Let's get a ride on a taxi." Rangi looked out to sea and gave a special low whistle.

They waited in the darkness.

"Looks like we're going to have to swim all the way." Jackson was in a hurry to get going. He began to walk out into the water. Then in the quietness, he heard a familiar whistle from out in the mist.

Fantastic. That would get them there much faster and save their energy. He gazed into the mist and soon two dark torpedoes emerged through the mist and swam swiftly towards them.

Jackson grinned from ear to ear as he wrapped his arms around the nearest dolphin. "Moko, how good to see you."

Rangi went over to the other dolphin and lay on it, giving it gentle strokes. "Oronui, haven't seen you for quite a while. It's so good to see you."

The dolphins were making their special little noises of pleasure.

Jackson lay down and held on to Moko. "Okay – let's go." They began to disappear into the mist. Rangi soon followed him on Oronui. They lay flat on the dolphins' backs, steering with gentle pressure from their knees. They moved swiftly and quietly through the water, out to sea, toward the boat.

Jackson watched the dark shape of the boat emerge through the fog. It had high sides. He couldn't see anyone on the deck. Thanks to the rain, if anyone was on board, they must be inside. He didn't see any ladders either or easy access on to the deck.

As they got closer, they pulled back on the dolphins, who stopped. They slipped off and swam quietly to the side of the boat. The waves, slopping against the hull of the boat, covered any sounds.

Jackson could feel the adrenaline pumping. "Let's split. I'll climb up the anchor chain and take a look. I'll signal if the coast is clear."

Rangi gave the thumbs-up and swam around to the other side. Jackson swam to the front of the boat and grasped the heavy metal chain with both hands. Swinging his legs over the chain, he climbed quickly up to the deck.

The chain swung around as the boat moved on the choppy sea, making climbing difficult. He got to the top of the anchor chain and reached up to the bottom rail on the deck. Quietly, he pulled himself onboard and slipped across under the shadow of some life rafts parked on the deck. He looked around the deck. Nothing was moving. It was empty, so he leaned over the edge of the boat and looked for Rangi. He spotted him waiting by the anchor chain and gave him a wave to signal the all-clear.

Rangi quickly followed him up the anchor chain and pulled himself onto the deck. As his feet let go of the chain it clanged noisily against the side of the boat. He moved quickly into the shadows at the front of the boat.

Jackson quickly pulled back into the shadows under the life raft. A cold chill ran down his back as a door at the other end of the boat's cabin burst open. One of the terrorists ran out, swinging a handgun from side to side as he searched the deck. There was a guard on duty.

Rangi wriggled along the deck in the shadows, toward another life raft. As he moved toward it, the man saw him.

He shouted, "Raise your hands and don't move!" The guard was twenty feet away, holding his gun with two hands, aiming it at Rangi. Jackson watched with horror as Rangi slowly stood up with his hands in the air. This was terrible. They mustn't get caught. There was no other way they could discover if Chappy was on the boat.

Suddenly Rangi looked out to sea and pointed. The guard turned to see what he was looking at. Rangi seized his opportunity. Crouching low, sucking air deep into his lungs, he raced forward, dived over the boat's rail and plunged into the sea. The guard spun around and fired three quick shots at him.

Rangi dived deep to avoid more bullets. Jackson knew he would have to surface soon for air. From their days spent together snorkeling in the bay he knew he only had three minutes max. But was Rangi okay? Had he been hit?

As Jackson lay quietly on the deck watching in the darkness, he called out to the Almighty One for help. "Lord, can you hear me? Please look after Rangi and keep us all safe," he pleaded. By now, Rangi's lungs would be screaming for air. He would have to find somewhere to surface.

From his position under the life raft, Jackson could see down the side of the boat towards the stern. The moon broke through the darkness. He thought he saw a shadow moving through the water behind the propeller housing. The shadow disappeared under the back of the boat. It must be Rangi. But what was that he could see streaming behind him? Was it blood?

As Jackson looked around for ideas, he was shocked. Three large black fish with delta fins were circling around the back of the boat. Sharks! Oh no – they must have been drawn by the smell of fresh blood in the water.

His best friend's blood!

23. DAY THREE 4:20 AM

Jackson lay under the life raft, wondering how they could ever get out of this mess. "Lord, quick, help us – we sure need it," he whispered.

He needed to quickly decide what to do. The guard was looking over the other side of the boat with his back to Jackson as he searched for Rangi. Now was the time for him to move.

Silently he crept along the deck, keeping the cabin between him and the guard. Staying low in the shadows, he searched around the side of the boat. He came to the back of the boat and slid silently into the cockpit. There were stairs leading down into the cabin.

Glancing along the boat, he could see the guard at the other end of the boat. He was still leaning over the rail, searching the water for Rangi. Jackson knew he didn't have much time. He moved, silent as a shadow, through the door, down four steps and into the cabin.

Except for a table and six chairs and a small kitchen at the other end, the cabin looked empty. A dim light revealed two doors near the kitchen. He crouched low and hurried to the other end. Slowly, he opened the left door. It was a bathroom. Jackson shut it and quickly and quietly opened the other door. The second room was dark. Using the light coming through the door, he saw six narrow bunks, lining the walls in two rows. He silently crept into the room to look around. Jackson almost jumped out of his skin when suddenly, something moved on one of the top bunks.

He looked into the darkness. There was a man lying on the top bunk. He must have been asleep. Jackson turned quickly to escape, then stopped abruptly. He had heard a grunt behind him. But the man hadn't moved. Jackson slowly turned back and looked up. It was difficult to see in the darkness, but he could make out that the man was gagged. His arms were tied to the bunk to immobilize him.

Suddenly he realized – it was Chappy!

He rushed back to the kitchen and grabbed a

knife from a drawer. The ropes were strong but he had soon cut Chappy free. Chappy sat up, rubbing his arms and legs. "So glad to see you arrive," he grinned.

Jackson warned him, "Quick – we've got to move fast. There's a guy on deck with a gun." Jackson led the way back through the main cabin, then onto the deck. The guard was still leaning over the rail at the other end of the boat.

"Dive deep and away!" Jackson cried, as he dived over the ship's rail into the sea. Chappy hit the water beside him. They disappeared into the cool black water. They surfaced a distance from the boat and began swimming away. A volley of shots sprayed the water around them. Luckily the bullets missed them. They were soon out of range.

Now the guard turned his attention on them. They urgently needed help. Jackson had to call up their water taxis, quickly. He gave their special whistle, hoping the dolphins were still close by. He looked around for Rangi, but couldn't see him. He must be somewhere. Surely he wasn't dead? Then with horror, Jackson saw Rangi lying on his side. He was swimming slowly toward them. Rangi was in trouble.

Jackson could see the dark shapes of several dorsal fins following him. They were in great danger. The sharks were closing in.

He looked up to check the boat. It seemed the guard had emptied his gun. Now he was making other plans. He was standing on the deck with a long, wicked-looking knife in his hand. Rangi watched as the man stuck the knife through his belt and dived overboard. The guard began swimming strongly toward them. He quickly began closing in on them.

Chappy looked like he was struggling. The time he had spent roped up on the bunk must have affected him. Maybe he was drugged? Jackson swam over to Rangi to help him. The guard was now only a few yards away.

He could see the sharks through the mist. They were following Rangi's trail of blood.

There was no sign of their dolphin friends.

24. DAY THREE 4:30 AM

Jackson swam alongside Rangi, pulling him along as fast as they both could go. He watched with horror as the guard closed in on Rangi and pulled the knife from his belt. An icy chill ran down his back as the bandit raised his knife over his best friend and prepared to plunge it down.

In desperation, Jackson used a karate kick and caught the guard in the stomach. That stopped him. But he was soon back. There was murder in his eyes. He raised his knife again. Without thinking, Jackson suddenly called out in desperation. "Lord, HELP US!"

The guard suddenly stopped swimming after them. He screamed as he turned around, wildly punching his knife into the water around him. Dark fins flashed. He screamed again. Within seconds, he had disappeared beneath the sea.

Jackson felt sick. They kept swimming as fast as they could. But they were still a long way from the beach, and Rangi was still bleeding. The sharks were swimming around them now. He was beginning to feel very tired. Swimming while holding Rangi up in the choppy sea was becoming more difficult. He looked around, but could see nothing but the sea. Chappy was now alongside, helping Jackson hold Rangi up.

Then Jackson heard a sound. It seemed like the music of angels. Could it be? Yes, now he could hear it more clearly, the squeaky whistles of Moko and Oronui. They had arrived.

The dolphins swam up to them. Then suddenly they turned away. For several minutes Jackson watched as the two dolphins dived, circled and plunged. They accelerated and traveled at incredible speed as they attacked the sharks. They had soon chased them away.

After a little while, they were back. Oronui came up underneath Rangi and gently nudged him. Rangi wrapped his arms around the dolphin and lay on her to rest his weary body. "How wonderful to see you again, my friend," he spoke into Oronui's ear.

Jackson was sure he could see Oronui smiling.

"Okay, our taxis have arrived." Rangi grinned as he turned to Chappy swimming close by.

"Incredible. I must be dreaming. I can't believe what I'm seeing. Just when I thought we were all goners!" Chappy gave him a big grin as he lay in the water, paddling on his back and resting. "Let's get moving back to shore."

Jackson turned to Rangi. "You ride in on Oronui and we'll follow on Moko."

Rangi whispered in Oronui's ear. The dolphin responded with a whistle. They soon disappeared into the mist, toward the shore.

"I bet you've never taken a dolphin taxi before." Jackson felt his spirits reviving as he maneuvered close to Moko.

"No, never have. If I wasn't seeing this I would never have believed it either." Chappy was smiling again.

Jackson leaned over Moko. "We need to link arms to ride back in on Moko. You come around the other side. Hold on tightly and we'll get a fast ride home."

Their biggest problem was hanging on. Moko

seemed to know they were in trouble. They held on with all their strength as Moko took off like an express train. They were halfway to the beach when Jackson saw the shadowy shape of the rowboat passing them in the mist on their right. One of the terrorists was bending over the oars.

They kept low in the water so they wouldn't be seen. Jackson decided the man must have heard the shots and was rowing out to the boat to check what had happened. The man didn't seem to see them or hear them with the noise of the waves crashing against the bow of the boat. He quickly disappeared into the mist behind them.

Rangi was waiting on the beach for them. He was talking to somebody. It was difficult to see them through the mist.

Jackson said goodbye to Moko who headed back out to sea. They moved quickly over. It was Jess. She was clinging to Rangi and weeping.

What could have happened?

25. DAY THREE 5:00 AM

Jackson hurried up the beach. Jess looked terrible. She threw herself at him, sobbing.

"They've got Sam."

"What? How? What happened?"

Jess needed a little while to calm down somewhat before she could talk. "Sam went down to the end of the beach to check out what was going on. They must've seen her. One of the men grabbed her and dragged her into the cave."

"Oh no! It's the last thing we needed right now. But first, can you help me fix Rangi's wound?" He found his clothes and tore a strip off the bottom of his T-shirt.

The waves crashing on the beach covered any sounds they made.

Jess looked at Rangi's arm and screamed.

"You're bleeding! I heard shots out at sea and I prayed that you would both be okay. Are you okay?"

"Yes, it's not too bad I guess. He got me in the arm. But I can still use it. The bone's not broken."

Then Jess saw Chappy approaching and screamed again. She ran over and wrapped her arms around him. "I can't believe that it's you. How wonderful to see you safe."

"I can't believe I'm here either. Everything seems like a big wonderful dream – especially riding in on the back of a dolphin." Chappy grinned. "I tell you, I've never felt happier in my life than when you guys rescued me! Those guys didn't plan to let me go alive."

Jackson slapped Chappy's back. "Chappy, it's so good to have found you and got you out of there. It's so good to have you back again."

"I'm eternally grateful you guys came and rescued me." Chappy repeated and smiled.

Their celebration was short-lived. Jessica had Rangi lie on the beach. "Thank the Lord he didn't hit you in the chest." She put her Girl Scout's first aid training into action and attended to his wound.

Soon his arm was strapped and tied tight. The

bandage was stained red but Jackson couldn't see any fresh blood coming through. Rangi tried using his arm carefully. It seemed he was very lucky. It must have only been a flesh wound.

Jackson paused and thought. Truly the Lord had been watching over them.

He was suddenly very serious. He turned to Chappy. "Right now we have a major problem." "Jess said Sam went down the end of the beach to check on what the terrorists were up to down there. It seems she got too close and was caught. They grabbed her and took her into the cave."

"Oh no! That's really bad news!" Chappy paused. "We'll use your cell phone and call the police immediately."

"Can't do that. There's no connection down here." Rangi grimaced.

"Oh, I forgot. You've got bikes. Rush home and call the police. I'll wait here."

Jackson leaned forward urgently. "Chappy, we're pretty sure we saw Sergeant Harris from the police station. He was in the cavern, meeting with the terrorists. If we call he could block any help. You're the only one who can call the police, and be sure to get through to the right person to get some action going.

"Best if you go, Chappy. Take my bike and call them from our farmhouse. If nobody's at home you'll find the door's open and the phone's on the kitchen table."

Chappy thought quickly. "Okay, I'll do it but I don't want to leave you here. You make sure you all stay out of sight and stay safe, okay? These guys are terrorists – they will stop at nothing."

"We'll stay safe."

Jackson wondered how they could stay safe and still help Sam. They couldn't leave her in there – she was in great danger.

It was still dark. The mist was still covering the beach, concealing them.

They crept to the top of the beach. Jackson found his bike and pulled it out of the bushes. Chappy took one of their flashlights, grabbed Jackson's bike and quickly disappeared into the darkness. The boys changed into their dry clothes. They sat together on the beach–in the darkness.

It seemed time stood still. They were sitting and waiting a long time but nothing was happening.

Jackson looked around at Rangi and Jessica. "We can't just sit here and leave Sam in there with those thugs. We need to get back into the cave and see what's happening. Maybe there's something we can do to help her."

"And we've gotta do it now."

26. DAY THREE 5:30 AM

Rangi went ahead as they crept through the forest. In the darkness it seemed to take forever to find the back entrance to the cave.

Jackson turned to Jess. "If it's okay with you, I think it would be better if just me and Boots go in right now. It'll be simpler and quieter. Why don't you wait out here to guide the others, when they arrive?"

"Huh, and let you two have all the fun." She gave a nervous laugh. "Okay, I'll wait out here and keep a lookout for the others arriving. I'll also be praying for you guys."

Jessica waited under the shelter of a large rimu tree. Jackson and Rangi crossed the river. Then they silently scrambled up the slippery slope in the darkness, to the back entrance of the cave.

They used Rangi's flashlight sparingly to conserve the batteries. It took them a little longer to find the entrance in the dark. Eventually they crept into the cave and paused.

Rangi scratched his head. "I sure hope the Lord knows where we are right now."

Jackson turned and looked at him. "Your granddad says He knows everything, so I guess He's looking after us. How about I use your flashlight and go ahead, seeing I gave mine to Chappy."

"Sounds good. Let's go."

Jackson went ahead into the cave. They were more familiar with the cave now and traveled faster, though working with one flashlight made it more difficult.

Jackson held the flashlight, pointing back to help Rangi and then stumbled over some rocks as he hurried. They immediately stopped – did the noise of the moving rocks warn the terrorists they were coming?

They waited in the darkness, listening for any noises. The only sound Jackson heard was the 'plop – plop' of water dripping from the ceiling. They moved on.

Eventually they came to the four big sinkholes in the cave floor. Jackson tapped Rangi on the shoulder. They stopped and Rangi waited while Jackson pulled the long piece of black baling twine out of his pocket. He crossed to the opposite side of the cave. Rangi held the flashlight as he tied one end firmly to a large stalagmite on the cave floor. He laid the twine across the floor and left the end lying by the small pile of rocks he had left on their last trip.

Rangi watched him with interest. "What's all this for, bro?"

"It could be our insurance policy," Jackson said grimly.

They went on at a slow but steady pace, creeping quietly around the stalagmites and loose rocks on the cave floor until Rangi suddenly stopped. They listened for a few minutes. Rough voices and curses of the terrorists echoed down the cave.

They were getting close.

Jackson whispered, "Lord, we sure could do with your help now."

Rangi added, "Hope He's listening. Okay, real quiet. Let's take a look."

There were three terrorists in the cavern. The other two must have been outside, with one on guard duty. Sergeant Harris wasn't in the cavern. Jackson could see a lot better now as he looked around. His eyes were more accustomed to the darkness.

There were automatic rifles stacked against the wall by the exit to the beach.

The two younger men were busy moving the last two large yellow crates away from the walls, preparing to carry them out. The older man was packing up their food and gear into a large box. Jackson could see Sam lying in the corner, trussed up with ropes. She looked uncomfortable lying on the rocks. She was gagged. Otherwise, she looked to be okay.

It looked as if the men were about finished and were getting ready to leave. They had to get Sam out of there quickly. From what Chappy had told them, they didn't take prisoners. Jackson guessed they were planning to take her with them.

They crouched in the shadows watching silently, waiting for an opportunity to rescue Sam.

Jackson was busy trying to figure out how they could all get out safely when the two younger men picked up their automatic rifles and slung them over their shoulders. "Okay – let's go."

They carefully picked up one of the crates at each end and marched out the exit toward the beach. Jackson and Rangi waited in the shadows, watching.

Then the older man put the lid on the box of camping gear. He swung it up onto his shoulder and turned to Sam.

He had a low, menacing voice. "Well I dunno what you're doing down here on the beach, my girl. But it's bad luck for you, my beauty. You're comin' with us and you'll be shark food tonight – just like the other fellow we caught."

He turned and carried the case of supplies out to the beach. Samantha was left alone in the flickering light.

"Quick – this is our chance. Let's go." Jackson was already on his feet, running across to Sam. Her eyes grew wide and brightened when she saw them. Jackson pulled out his pocket knife and began slicing through the ropes, while Rangi undid her gag. Sam stumbled to her feet. She was unsteady from lying cramped on the cave floor.

"Let's run for it," Jackson hissed. "Those guys will be back real soon to take the last crate." They turned and raced across the cavern to the back entrance.

Halfway across, the silence was suddenly shattered by one of the terrorists and a deafening burst of gunfire. A volley of bullets bounced around the walls sending chips of rocks flying, followed by a shout.

"Stop! Put your hands above your heads or you're all dead meat."

A thunderous second volley of automatic gunfire into the ceiling brought down a shower of stones and small rocks.

Jackson, Rangi and Sam stopped in the middle of the cavern. Jackson's pulse was racing. His ears were ringing from the noise.

He thought about running for it. But there was no way they would make it. It was another four yards and with those automatic rifles, they couldn't miss.

They slowly raised their hands in the air, and turned around. The two younger terrorists stood watching them with their automatic rifles raised, fingers ready on the triggers. There was no escape.

It was so cruel. They had been so close to disappearing down the cave to safety. Now the three of them were caught.

Now there was no escape.

"On the floor – face down." One of the terrorists came across and used his rifle to prod them to the floor. Reluctantly they lay down on the floor. They were securely tied and gagged. Then they were dragged across the cavern floor and dumped painfully in a heap in the corner.

One of the men snarled at them, "Thought you were clever. Well we've got all of you now – white pigs. When we get you out to sea you'll be sorry you interfered. One more crate to go, load the boat and we'll be back for you." He kicked Rangi in the stomach. Rangi groaned. They picked up the last crate and quickly marched out toward the beach.

Jackson felt sick. A wave of despair swept over him. Nothing could save them now. The ropes were tied very tightly. He could feel them biting into his legs and arms. He looked at the others. He couldn't move or talk.

It would be at least another half hour, maybe longer, before the police arrived. The terrorists were moving quickly. They would be gone. Disappearing into the mist – with Jackson, Sam and Rangi on board.

Then he remembered.

He looked up at the roof of the cavern and prayed.

27. DAY THREE 6:30 AM

Rangi was wriggling and making noises behind his gag. Jackson rolled over painfully. He could barely move his arms or legs. The police would take at least another thirty or forty minutes. The terrorists would be back at any time now. He lay in the semi-darkness trying desperately to think how he could get free.

If only he could move – but the ropes were so tight they were cutting into his arms and legs. They were surely done for. Would the terrorists shoot them before taking them out to the boat? He decided they would want them to walk out to save having to carry them.

Jackson stiffened. He had heard a noise. Some rocks had moved. It came from the cave leading out to the back entrance.

A shiver went down his spine. Someone else was there.

They must have been back already. He couldn't turn his head to see who, or what, it was. He waited, sweating.

With a surge of energy, he lifted his body, turned over to face the cavern, and waited for the end.

28. DAY THREE 6:35 AM

A shadowy figure darted across the cavern toward them. Then he heard a familiar voice whisper.

"Looks like you guys need some help."

It was his little sister Jess – brave as a trooper. She must have come into the cave looking for them.

All he could do was mumble into his gag. Jess quickly got to work. She pulled out her pocket knife. It was sharp and she soon cut through the ropes and gags.

Jackson was the first one who could speak. "The terrorists will be back any second. Run for it." The four of them turned and ran for the cave leading out to the back entrance.

They were halfway across the cavern floor when they heard one of the terrorists shout, "Stop – now!

Okay, you're dead meat. Die!" Another volley of automatic gunfire whistled over their heads, chipping stones, showering them with small rocks.

Jackson smashed a fist into the palm of his hand. The terrorists were back. They must have left the crate on the beach and come back quickly. Jackson couldn't believe their bad luck.

One of the terrorists shouted, "Stop. Now!

They fired another volley into roof of the cavern to make them stop. But this time the hail of bullets into the roof suddenly opened a large hole in the cavern roof and brought down a massive rockfall.

Clouds of thick dust filled the air. Large boulders bounced across the floor.

"Quick! Run for the cave. Don't stop!" Jackson stepped aside and waited as the others rushed past – then followed them as fast as he could. He was having trouble breathing – the air was thick with choking dust and gunfire smoke.

They crouched low to avoid the automatic gunfire as they ran around the corner and stumbled into the darkness of the cave.

29. DAY THREE 6:40 AM

Rangi led the charge down the cave, his flashlight beam bouncing around the walls and floor. Sam followed close behind him, then Jess with her flashlight.

Jackson followed, stumbling along in the semidarkness, desperately trying to see the rocky floor. The thunderous noise from the rifles and ricocheting bullets was terrifying.

They had only run a short distance when the dazzling light of a spotlight shone down the cave from behind them. It lit up the cave ahead of them, helping them to see better. But now they were easy targets.

Jackson flinched as the terrorists opened fire again. It was deafening. Bullets whistled past their heads, ricocheting off the cave walls, spraying them with sharp chips of rock.

They dived through a group of rocky stalagmites for protection.

Jackson shouted into the darkness, "Keep your head down, crouch and watch your feet!" He stumbled along the rocky cave floor. "Lord, we need your help NOW!"

The spotlight went out for a few seconds and the shooting stopped. The terrorists were having problems too. Then the spotlight came on again and the bullets started flying around them. They rounded a bend in the cave.

It seemed they were safe for a while. Jackson suddenly stumbled over some loose rocks. He wrenched his ankle sharply. He felt the hot pain run up his leg.

Jackson hobbled along as fast as he could. The others began to get further ahead. It was becoming impossible to see without a flashlight. All of a sudden his blood ran cold. He thought he saw his pile of rocks ahead as Rangi's flashlight bounced over them. The sink holes! He shouted a warning to Jess – but he was too late.

Jackson watched with horror as Jess headed

straight for one of the sinkholes.

Ignoring the pain in his ankle, he leapt ahead. He saw her slip on the edge and fall.

Jackson desperately rushed forward. He grabbed at her with one arm.

His fingers found her belt and held on as Jess fell into the sinkhole.

His feet were sliding on wet rock. Jessica's weight was dragging him into the hole with her. He cried out again, "Lord, help me save her!"

His front foot suddenly caught in a crevice near the edge of the sinkhole, giving him a grip. Calling on all of his strength, he managed to swing Jess around and back up onto the cave floor. His ankle was now desperately sore and swollen. He couldn't go on. Jess shouted, "Thanks, big brother!" and took off to catch the others. Jackson dived into a dark crevice in the rock wall of the cave and collapsed on the floor.

He could hear the terrorists closing in. His only chance of survival now was that they wouldn't see him crouching inside the crevice.

He squeezed back into the crevice. Their shouting and the clatter of their boots was getting closer.

They were firing bursts of bullets down the cave; but the gang was sheltered by the twists and turns of the cave ahead.

Then the spotlight shone brightly around him. An icy-cold shiver ran down his spine as the terrorists arrived around the corner.

He squeezed hard back into the narrow crevice, and waited.

30. DAY THREE 6:45 AM

Jackson felt something prickly under his hand. He quickly pulled his hand away. Then he remembered! It was the length of black rope he had left lying on the cave floor. Was it too late to use it?

In a flash, he grabbed it and wrapped it around his arm. Then, pulling back as hard as he could, he braced himself against a rock as they came running towards him. One of the terrorists saw him and, with an evil smile, swung his automatic rifle around at him as he ran. The spotlight lit him up. Jackson froze as he saw the man's finger hovering over the trigger.

Without warning, the terrorist's foot hit the taut rope and he catapulted into the air. His gun chattered away, spraying bullets into the roof of the cave as he fell into the sinkhole. The other two men were close behind.

Jackson's arm ached with the effort as he leaned back hard and watched as they skidded on the damp rocky cave floor, desperately trying to stop. They were slowing down and turning toward him when the first man hit the black rope and began to sway forward, calling out to his friend to catch him. The man behind him dropped his gun. It clattered to the rocky floor as he reached out to grab his friend's hand.

He was bracing himself to pull the first man back from the hole when he hit the rope himself and tumbled forward. They fell together into the darkness, shouting curses and yelling with pain as they hit the rocks below.

Jackson sat in the darkness for a minute trying to calm his mind.

He whistled loudly and called to the others. "Can someone come back with a flashlight and get me out of here? They've fallen into a sinkhole."

There was a long silence. Then Rangi's voice floated back down the cave. "Hey, bro! What are you doing back there?"

A few moments later, Rangi turned a corner in

the cave and saw Jackson sitting on the cave floor in the dark, with his swollen ankle stretched out. "Oh boy, you've sure done your ankle in. It looks real bad."

Rangi leaned over the edge of the sinkhole and flashed his light down. He leaped back quickly as a hail of bullets flew past his ear. "They sure are an unfriendly lot." He grinned at Jackson. "Say, that rope came in handy, bro!"

Jackson got up slowly and, leaning hard on Rangi, he staggered along on his good foot. The two of them slowly made their way back along the rocky floor of the cave toward the entrance.

Rangi wiped blood from his face where chips of rock had hit him. He grinned. "Think I've had enough excitement for today."

What else could go wrong?

31. DAY THREE 7:00 AM

Jackson winced. His ankle was throbbing with each step. He longed to sit down. The pain in his ankle was so bad he almost forgot Rangi's bullet wound. It took them a long time to reach the exit from the cave. At last, they slowly climbed out. Jackson rubbed his eyes in the bright sunshine.

He was stunned.

He could hear a crowd of people cheering.

What were all those people doing standing, waiting on the other side of the river?

He could see Jess and Sam standing under the trees talking to two police officers. His mom and dad and some of their neighbors were standing, watching and waiting. When they saw them coming down the hillside from the cave they all cheered and whistled loudly.

Two police officers ran over to help Jackson through the bush and down the hillside to the clearing by the river. He saw Sergeant Harris waiting too. His hands were handcuffed behind his back.

Two police helicopters sat in the clearing. The Armed Offenders Squad stood waiting on the bank.

One of them stepped forward. He was wearing a cluster of stripes on his arm. "Boys, you've done a fantastic job and we're so proud of you both. Mr. Chapman has told us about the situation. We need to round up these fellows promptly. Now quickly, tell me where they are – and what happened, so we can move in."

Jackson let Rangi do the talking, while he sat down on the ground. He was too sore and too tired. Rangi explained how they had been held captive in the cave deep under the mountain; how Jess had come in alone and cut them loose; how the three terrorists had been chasing them through the cave trying to kill them and how Jackson had trapped them in a sinkhole.

"Unless they've managed to climb the sheer rock walls, you'll find them sitting at the bottom of a twelve-foot sinkhole ten minutes back. The walls are so sheer even a 'possum couldn't climb them.

"Don't poke your nose over the edge like I did. They are heavily armed and will try to shoot your heads off."

Jackson added, "We think another terrorist has rowed out to their boat. It's parked two hundred yards offshore. They've been loading crates of stuff into the boat and were about ready to leave."

The Armed Offenders Squad moved quickly up the hill and into the cave. The dazzling light from their flashlights disappeared into the cave.

Jackson's mom was beside him. "We'll have to bandage your ankle and we need to get you both home to get your injuries fixed." She wiped her eyes. "Just to think you all could have been killed. Thank God you're all safe."

Rangi grinned at them. "That was some adventure eh – and we've still got the rest of the summer holidays to see what else turns up."

They all laughed and high-fived. Rangi used his other arm.

"Sure is good to be out in one piece." Jackson looked around at them. "For a while I thought we were going to be toast."

He turned around and looked at Jess. "Jess, you were amazing coming into the cavern to rescue us. Am I glad to have such a great sister as you. We sure owe you a lot."

Jess put an arm around her brother. "That's okay, big brother. When you hadn't showed up on time, I decided I needed to go in and see what you were all up to." They laughed.

Jackson noticed his dad was standing with his arm around his mom. It seemed a long time since he had seen that happen.

They all piled into Jackson's dad's old Land Rover and headed back to the farm.

Chappy sat in the back with The Riwaka Gang. "I've never been happier in my life to see someone arrive than when you two arrived on the boat." He gave a huge smile as he leaned back, relaxing. "You guys are the best. Thanks, I owe you a lot."

Jackson was feeling very contented. "I guess we've got to say the same. Rangi and I have never been happier to see anyone than when we found you on that boat."

Rangi leaned forward. "You know – with the triathlon coming up, we had to find our coach!"

The Land Rover echoed with their laughter as they turned up the driveway to the house.

32. DAY THREE - THE PARTY!

They settled into chairs on the veranda. Jackson had never been so happy to get home.

"Looks like you're going to miss the race." Sam looked at Jackson for a minute, then poked his ankle.

"Ouch. Easy on, that hurts."

"Just testing." She smiled.

Granddad Kingi pulled up in his old Toyota van and sat with them. "I heard the news about you all on the grapevine. What a time you've had. I'm so grateful to see you all made it back safe and sound." He gave each of them a shoulder hug.

Jackson turned and looked at Granddad. "It was a real scary time. But the Lord really did help us when we needed it. It was so amazing."

"Yeah, it was really cool. Even when I was all

tied up I just knew somehow it was going to turn out okay." Sam looked up at her grandfather. Her eyes were shining. "Thank you, Granddad."

"Well...you all remember it's not only when you're in trouble. The Lord is always there with you."

Jackson's dad spoke up. "Your mom and I have been talking. I can see I need to rearrange my time so I'm home some more. I'm going to begin working on this right away."

His mom beamed at his dad. "Jack, I'm so pleased to hear you say that. I'm so blessed to have you for my man." She gave him a long kiss. The Riwaka Gang whooped and wolf whistled in delight.

Several carloads of people pulled up. Jackson recognized their headmaster, the town mayor and others and wondered why they were all there.

His dad had fired up the barbecue on the veranda. Jackson loved the smell of the steaks grilling with the onions, tomatoes and all the trimmings.

"What's all the fuss about?" he asked.

"Your mom and I decided to put on a special feast to celebrate." He ruffled Jackson's hair. "I'm mighty proud of you, son, and your friends too."

Granddad gave thanks to the Lord for the meal and for their safe return. Everyone tucked in.

After they had cleared away the plates, their headmaster stood up and gave a short speech thanking them for rescuing Chappy.

The Commissioner of Police stood up. "I don't know how these young fellows managed to catch those terrorists when Interpol, the international police force, couldn't."

He looked around at them all and grinned. "You young folk are heroes and we are all very proud of you."

He told them the terrorists were members of an international terrorist gang. They were on Interpol's 'most dangerous and most wanted list'.

The crates in the cavern contained thorium pentoxide, a new compound used for advanced nuclear bombs, ten times more powerful than any bomb ever made. The terrorists had smuggled it from the uranium mines in Australia.

They had planned to use it to destroy cities in the Western world.

Millions of lives had been saved because of the

bravery of The Riwaka Gang.

There was an international reward for capturing these terrorists. He asked The Riwaka Gang to step forward. Jackson, Jessica, Rangi and Samantha lined up. He shook their hands and presented Jackson with a check. Jackson looked at it and gasped. $150,000! Good grief! What would they do with so much money?

Then Granddad stood. It suddenly became quiet. Granddad Kingi was highly respected by everyone in the valley.

"I agree with everything that's been said. These are outstanding young people and they have done a wonderful effort of bravery, resulting in the capture of these terrorists. Well done, Rangi, Jackson, Samantha and Jessica, we are so proud of you. You have proved what can be done through courage, good thinking and faith in yourselves as well as the Almighty God, who watches over us."

The gang got together to discuss the reward. Then Jackson stood, leaning on his crutches.

"We've decided how to use the reward money. Mostly we want to use the money for our school and for our town. We've decided to give $80,000 to complete our school's gymnasium and $50,000 to build a youth drop-in centre in town where we can all hang out and do special stuff. We'll use the other $20,000 to build a clubhouse for The Riwaka Gang by the beach, at the bottom of our farm." He sat down as they all cheered and clapped.

Then they were all quiet again as Jessica stood up.

"I'm really proud of my big brother, but there's just one thing I wanted to say to him." She turned, looked at Jackson and smiled.

"Any time you get into trouble again and need saving, just give me a call." Jackson laughed and gave her a hug as they all cheered.

Sam turned to them. "Know what? I can feel another adventure coming."

Life is a great adventure!
Live it with confidence and with faith.
Denis Shuker

A message from Denis Shuker, writer, and friend of The Riwaka Gang:

I have been talking with the gang and they want me to tell you – don't miss their next adventure coming out about the middle of 2013.

They said to tell you their next adventure was even wilder and scarier than Shark Bay. They also told me to not tell you any of the details, because it would spoil the story when you read the book. Jackson said you've got to sign up to make sure you get information about the book to know when it's finished, and they'll tell you a bit about the story too.

To sign up for information you need to go to my web address:

www.denisshuker.com

Just put in your name and email address and I'll send you some good stuff about the book and when it's going to be ready. You will also get some other special stuff about the book as well.

But you must sign up or you won't know when the book comes out as it will be on www.amazon.com – not in your local bookstore.

The gang had a great time after all the celebrations you read about at the end of this book. They are excited about their new clubhouse and are busy working on plans for it. They are already talking with their dads and friends about helping put the framing up. They asked me to go and help too but I had to tell them I can't write their new adventure if I'm helping build the clubhouse. But I will go when they finish it, to have a look and help them celebrate. It's going to be looking over the beach, at the bottom of the Curtis's farm. Rangi said it will be a good place to store their surfboards and snorkeling gear too.

But I must be careful not to say too much or I might begin to tell you about the next adventure. Then it wouldn't be a surprise for you when you read it. I'm really excited about this next book and I know you will be too.

So remember to go to my website and sign up for information and news about the book. Sam said she thinks we ought to have competitions as well. The gang can work on the details and I'll put them on my website for you to have fun with.

So go to: www.denisshuker.com now and sign up for information before you forget.

Jessica called out that I need to tell you:

If you like the book, <u>write a review</u> on the Amazon page (where you bought it) and click a bunch of stars. Nothing fancy needed, just one or two sentences about why you liked it would be great. That will help other kids when they are thinking about buying the book.

Thanks a bunch – you've been a great reader and I look forward to getting in touch again after you have signed up. We are all off to the beach now – the surf is up.

Bye – see you next time. Until then have fun and stay safe.

    –   Denis Shuker,

        Friend of The Riwaka gang.

About the Author —

Denis Shuker is a retired, country pharmacist and missionary. He has worked in many countries and now lives in Auckland, New Zealand. Happily married, he has four children, plus a bunch of grandchildren. His favorite interests include racing his Laser yacht, mountaineering, camping and hiking in the mountains. Denis was a Scout Leader for many years and helped organize camps, hikes, river rafting, snow caving and other great adventures with an enthusiastic group of young people.

He is currently working on more thrilling adventures of THE RIWAKA GANG. You won't want to miss these. Look for his books on **www.amazon.com**

Search for: **The Riwaka Gang** or **Denis Shuker**.

For tons of information about new books coming up — more about The Riwaka Gang and New Zealand, go to:

www.denisshuker.com and sign up.

Made in the USA
Middletown, DE
14 December 2017